T0014605

Readers love ANDREW GREY

New Leaf

"For the majority, the story is like going for a walk in your favorite park… a pleasant excursion allowing for reflection and figuring out a way forward with life."

—Love Bytes

"If you like ex-police officers, ex-actors, hurt/comfort, with a touch of mystery and suspense and some mild man-sex you will love this one."

—TTC Books and More

Rescue Me

"Grey certainly captures the 'spark when a dog and person click,' as well as the attraction between Mitchell and Beau…"

—*Publishers Weekly*

"This was a beautiful story of overcoming abuse, of two men who each want to be in a loving relationship and have to put the past in the past."

—Paranormal Romance Guild

By ANDREW GREY

By ANDREW GREY (CONT.)

Published by DREAMSPINNER PRESS
www.dreamspinnerpress.com

ANDREW GREY

SECOND GO-ROUND

Published by
DREAMSPINNER PRESS

5032 Capital Circle SW, Suite 2, PMB# 279,
Tallahassee, FL 32305-7886 USA
www.dreamspinnerpress.com

This is a work of fiction. Names, characters, places, and incidents either
are the product of author imagination or are used fictitiously, and any
resemblance to actual persons, living or dead, business establishments,
events, or locales is entirely coincidental.

Second Go-Round
© 2022 Andrew Grey

Cover Art
© 2022 L.C. Chase
http://www.lcchase.com
Cover content is for illustrative purposes only and any person depicted
on the cover is a model.

Mass Market Paperback ISBN: 978-1-64108-257-0
Trade Paperback ISBN: 978-1-64405-960-9
Digital ISBN: 978-1-64405-959-3
Mass Market Paperback published June 2022
v. 1.0

Printed in the United States of America

Chapter 1

DUSTIN MEYERS woke alone in bed to the sound of a familiar pair of cowboy boots thunking on the floor down the hall. He could almost see his former rodeo-riding partner of more than twenty years, Marshall Brand, stomping through the kitchen in that way he had. The man never did anything by halves, and that included attacking his breakfast like it was going to expire in sixty seconds.

Unfortunately it meant that when Marshall was awake, so was the rest of the fucking house. It had been endearing at one time, especially since the two of them had christened that kitchen table more than once on a cool Dallas spring morning. But they hadn't done that in a long time.

Dustin got out of bed and shuffled into the kitchen. "What's got you stomping like one of them damned bulls you used to ride?" he asked, pulling open the refrigerator door to grab the juice. He poured a glass and downed it to get his body going. There had been a time when coffee, the lifeblood of any ranch, would be what he first reached for, but the years had taken their toll, and drinking coffee anymore only meant the caffeine jitters rather than a pick-me-up… and most of the time the jolt of sugar had the same effect.

"Fucking fences got knocked down by some stupid city people who have no idea how to fucking drive when there aren't lights every ten damned feet to show them where to go. They claim they saw a cow cross in front of them and it ran them off the road. But the only hole in the fence was the one they made. I think the guy was drinking, because there ain't no pink cows in this part of Texas, outside of Dallas pride anyway." His lips curled into a brief smile, but the scowl was back fast enough.

"Okay. Give me two seconds to get dressed and I'll meet you in the yard." Dustin turned and hurried back to the bedroom. He pulled on jeans and a shirt, some socks, and then his boots, then grabbed his hat and gloves on his way out the back door. Pal, Dustin's German shepherd shadow, was waiting by the truck door. Marshall scowled again, but Dustin ignored it and pulled open the door to let Pal jump in before he climbed inside and pulled the old door closed. "Let's go. Have you called the guys?"

Marshall humphed as he threw the truck in gear, and they barreled down the drive and made the left turn at the road. Dustin held on to Pal even though he had his seat restraint on. Marshall sped up. Dustin had never understood why every time Marshall got into any type of moving vehicle, he drove like a bat out of hell. There was never any other speed, just full-out go for broke. Dustin held the "oh shit" handle with his right hand and Pal with his left as Marshall braked hard at the blockade of cattle across the road. Damn, there had to be a hundred of them milling around.

Engines rumbled in the distance, and soon two red ATVs appeared over the slight rise to the south. The annoying sounds had some of the cattle swinging their heads toward the screech, and they began moving away, thankfully back through the broken fence. Others followed, and soon enough their break for freedom became a move back toward captivity and the grass the beasts lived on.

Willy, the youngest of the hands, drove the rest of the meandering herd through the break in the fence, and then he followed, sending the cattle farther into the pasture, away from the hole, while Patrick stayed outside in case any of the cattle tried to make a break for it.

"How many did you pass?" Marshall growled as though the break in the fence was Patrick's fault. Of course it wasn't, and Patrick, after working for Marshall for four years, ignored his snippy tone and kept to business. It was Dustin who took exception to the way Marshall acted, and he clenched his hand once before forcing it to relax. There was no use having a fight right out here in front of the hands and the damned cattle.

"A dozen or so," Patrick answered. "They're clustered together about a mile over that way." He seemed about as thrilled about this as Dustin was, but shit like this happened on a ranch.

"Leave me the supplies and I'll start getting the old stuff down and out. You all bring in our wayward babies, and then we can close this up and secure it." Dustin called Pal, and Marshall helped him get the supplies out of the back of the truck. Then he took off with Patrick and Willy to round up the others, the engines growing quieter in the distance.

The cattle settled back into their area, munching away, so Dustin began cutting away the damaged wire, rolling it, and bundling it. He set it well out of the way as Pal guarded the opening like a sentry in case any of the large beasts came exploring. Pal was an amazing dog—smart, loyal to a fault, and he knew his job. He was also Dustin's best friend. He usually slept on the floor right beside Dustin's bed, and he was always there, following Dustin through much of his day, unless Marshall needed him, and then Pal went to work with him. "Watching to keep us safe," Dustin said to Pal as he checked each of the fence posts. Then he groaned and grabbed a shovel when he realized he'd have to dig out the weakened ones. This part always took the longest and was the hardest, especially as the sun rose higher in the sky. Still, the job wasn't going to do itself.

Dustin banged his gloves together to knock off the dirt and started digging. The soil held the bent posts tight, and it took work to get them free. He'd managed two of them by the time the sound of engines drew nearer. Dustin called Pal, and they moved out of the way as the mini cattle herd approached, driven by the truck and ATVs. Fortunately the cattle seemed to understand where they were going, because they didn't balk. They just went right through the opening to join the others.

"Is that all?" Dustin asked.

"Think so. We checked around and didn't see any more," Willy answered. "Followed the tracks, and we think they stayed together." He wiped his brow with the back of his hand. "I sure hope so."

"Has anyone called?" Marshall asked, and Dustin checked his phone just in case before shaking his head. "Well, that's a blessing, anyway." He sighed, and for a second the sun caught the side of his face. Dustin's mind filled in the spaces in between, and Marshall appeared the way he had when Dustin first met him. It had been in a situation similar to this, rounding up some cattle. Marshall had been almost majestic back then. "Patrick, help Dustin, will ya? Willy and I will make another pass just to be sure we didn't miss any." And just like that, the illusion popped and Dustin was back to the here and now.

There had been a time when Marshall would never have thought twice about staying. The two of them used to be inseparable, but now it seemed they were about as separate as two people could be when they still lived in the same house. Not that they fought or yelled at each other or anything like that. They just seemed to be living separate lives.

When Dustin was a kid, his father had taken them all on vacation, and at one point, he had pulled over to the side of the road and pointed at two white lines that cut through the land toward the horizon. "That's the Santa Fe Trail," his dad had said. Dustin remembered nodding, wondering how the lines from the wagons all those years ago could still be there. "Those ruts cut deep, and nature hasn't filled them in yet," his dad had said in answer to the question.

Now, as Marshall leapt onto the ATV like an excited kid—excitement that used to be directed at Dustin, but now always seemed to lead away—it was another one of those times when all Dustin could see were the deep ruts, like those of the trail, leading off behind Marshall. The worst part was that he had no idea how to fix them. They always seemed to pull the two of them along the same paths they'd always traveled.

"Dustin," Patrick said, and he pulled himself out of his own thoughts.

"Sorry." He began hauling the waste fencing to the truck and tossing it in the back. Then he and Patrick set to work placing the new posts and stringing the wire. The task went smoothly with the two of them, and soon enough they had everything loaded in the back. Dustin called Pal, who jumped in the cab.

"What's going on at the old Hartier place?" Dustin asked as he pulled toward the road. "That house has been empty for almost ten years."

"Looks like workmen," Patrick said. "I heard in the coffee shop yesterday that the Hartier estate had finally been settled and the house had been sold. I guess the rumors were right for once." Patrick patted Pal on the back, then stroked his head. "It seems the owners are fixing up the place before they move in."

"That's good," Dustin said, turning left instead of right.

"Whatcha doing?" Patrick asked.

"Just being nosey. Besides, we can check down this way to make sure there aren't any strays." Dustin wasn't above using the excuse of finding stray cattle to see what was going on. "It won't take long, and then I'll feed everyone."

"Muffins?" Patrick asked with a smile while Dustin slowed as he drove past the house. Two trucks and a van were parked in front of the old house, with ladders propped up against the front. Two men worked with sprayers to change the color to cool gray. "I like it."

Dustin nodded. "Me too." He pulled into the drive and got out. "Pal, stay," he said. He rolled the windows down the whole way so he would have plenty of air. Pal would stick his head out, but he'd do what he was told.

"Can I help you?" A woman in jeans and a blouse that clung to her, probably from the heat, came out of the house. She pulled the fabric away from her skin.

"Yes, sorry. I didn't mean to interrupt you. I'm Dustin, and I live up the road. You could say that my partner Marshall and I are your neighbors. We had some fence go down and I saw activity, so I thought I'd ask if you'd seen any cattle wander through." It was a little flimsy, but she smiled and shook her head.

"Nothing like that. One of the guys found a clutch of snakes that we took care of, and there seems to be a possum that's tried to take up residence near the wood pile. I think we might even have bats that we're clearing out, carefully, but no cattle." Dustin liked her. "Sorry. I'm Anne, and my husband,

Richard, took the kids to town so they could spend a little while in the air-conditioning." She turned to the side of the house. "The old one here worked yesterday, but that was obviously its last hurrah." She wiped her hair back.

"Do you need Patrick to look at it? He's good with that sort of thing." Dustin turned, but Patrick was already marching to the truck. He grabbed a toolbox and headed across the scrubby yard toward the unit.

"He doesn't need to do that. I was about to call someone," Anne said, but Dustin shrugged.

"We help our neighbors, and if Patrick can't fix it, he can call his dad for you. Between them, they keep all those sorts of thing running for us."

Anne seemed to deflate right in front of him. "I'd appreciate it so much. The heat and humidity are like nothing I'm used to." Her smile went most of the way to her eyes, which had a few more lines than Dustin would have suspected for someone her age. Still, she was pretty, even if she had been working hard and was covered in a sheen of sweat. "Not that I don't know what Texas summers are like. But being without air-conditioning with two kids is just one of those trials, I guess."

"I got it." Patrick waved as he headed for the front door. He disappeared for a second and then came back out. He closed the door most of the way before heading over. "It was a bad connection. I was able to fix it, and the house seems to be cooling. But the unit is really old, so I'd have someone replace it."

Anne sighed. "I figured we'd have to do that, but at least the house can be cool. Dustin said your father does this kind of work?" She already seemed more relaxed. Patrick handed her a card. "Thank you so much for your help. Is there anything I can get you?"

Patrick shook his head. "Glad I could help." He lifted his hat and headed to the truck with the toolbox. Anne turned back to Dustin.

"Are you sure I can't offer you some coffee or something cold to drink?" she asked, already turning toward the house.

"Thank you, but I need to get back and check in to make sure that our cattle are all where they should be." He lifted his hat with a smile the way he had always been taught. "It was good to meet you, and I'm sure we'll be seeing you all around." He was turning, intending to leave, when a gray Volvo wagon pulled in and slowly rolled up to the house. Dustin smiled and waited as a man got out and helped the two boys out of the back.

"Can I help you?" he asked a little warily.

"Richard, this is Dustin. He and his partner are our neighbors." Anne seemed tired. Richard's smile brightened, and some of the tension left him. They shook hands, and Dustin motioned to Patrick, who joined them.

"And you must be Dustin's partner?" Richard said as Patrick approached.

"No. I'm one of their hands. Dustin and Marshall own the ranch."

"Patrick was able to get the air-conditioning working," Anne said, and Richard's eyes lit up.

"Oh, thank you so much." He shook Patrick's hand with both of his. "You're a godsend." He released Patrick's hand and his smile grew wider. "Since the house is cooling, can we get you anything?"

"A doggie!" one of the boys cried, and just like that, Pal jumped out of the now open truck door and raced over to the porch.

"Pal, stop," Dustin called. Pal stopped running so abruptly he skidded forward in the dirt on his butt. He turned, probably wondering what he had done wrong, mouth hanging open in the heat.

"Boys…," Anne cautioned, the pitch of her voice rising fast.

"Pal is great," Dustin said quickly. "He's super friendly and he wouldn't hurt anyone." As if to prove the point, Pal inched forward and paused at the edge of the porch. Anne relaxed, and the boys came forward. Pal lifted his head and slowly climbed onto the porch as though he expected to be scolded any second. "Pal, come back here."

"Anne," Richard said softly, and she nodded. The boys walked closer, and Pal rolled over. That seemed to be the icebreaker. The boys sat down to pet Pal, who soaked up the attention like a sponge.

"I'm sorry," Dustin said. He hadn't wanted to cause any trouble.

"It's okay," Richard said, taking Anne's hand.

"Yeah. It's okay." Color rose in her cheeks. "I'm…." She seemed to reconsider what she was going to say. "The boys sure like him."

"Pal has been with me since he was a pup, ten years ago. He just loves attention and children, as

you can see." Pal was still on his back as the boys
rubbed his belly.

"Where are my manners?" Anne asked. "Our
older son, Oliver, is seven, and the younger one, who
just ended up on his four-year-old butt, is Noah."
She smiled now, and Richard did the same. Pal rolled
over and sat next to the boys, who petted him no end.
It was a wonderful scene, and Dustin watched the
boys as they played. He sighed and tried to keep the
sound to himself. The past was the past, and it needed to stay there.

"Okay," Richard said, and both boys looked up.
"Mr. Dustin probably needs to go, and we all need to
get inside where it's cooler." They stood and backed
away from Pal. Dustin patted his leg, and Pal hurried
over and sat next to him. "Can you say thank you?"
Richard asked.

"Thank you, Pal," both boys called. Richard and
Anne seemed flummoxed, but Dustin just smiled.

"I'm glad you both got to meet him." He turned
to Anne and Richard. "It was so good to meet you
both. We're right up the road about a mile. If you
need anything, let us know." He gave Richard one
of the ranch cards with their number on it. "I don't
want to keep you any longer, but I hope we'll see
you again."

"Can we play with Pal sometime?" Noah asked.
"He's a nice doggie."

"I think he'd really like that." Dustin didn't want
to speak for the boy's parents and hoped he gave a
proper answer.

"Yes. We should be able to arrange that," Richard said, lifting Oliver into his arms, and Anne did the same with Noah. Dustin and Patrick returned to the truck, and Pal jumped right in. Dustin waved and then backed out of the drive. He made the turn home and tried not to let his old hopes overwhelm him. The decisions he'd made couldn't be undone, and whatever reasons he'd had, regretting them wasn't going to change anything. Pal lay on the seat, resting his head in Dustin's lap as though he could read Dustin's mind. Not that it would do any of them any good. But still, Dustin couldn't get his mind back where it belonged.

Chapter 2

"WHERE HAVE you been?" Marshall asked as the truck pulled into the yard. He had been starting to wonder if something was wrong. Everyone else had returned from hunting for any stray cattle, but Dustin hadn't come home. Marshall had found himself returning to the front of the ranch to check the drive every five minutes, and now Dustin coming home like nothing had happened pissed him off.

Dustin got out of the truck, and Pal bounded after him.

Patrick grabbed the tools and a load of the used fencing and headed off toward the work shed. Marshall knew the tone he'd used and that the guys had learned to avoid him when he used it. He probably shouldn't talk to Dustin like that, but he was worried, and it just came out.

"I met our new neighbors," Dustin answered, and Marshall tilted his head. Nothing ever seemed to faze him. Dustin just seemed to let everything wash over him and flow away rather than getting angry in return.

"What new neighbors?" Marshall asked. Dusty's answer had taken him by surprise. "I haven't seen anyone." He wondered what he'd missed. Marshall hated to be taken by surprise about anything. It was his job to see to it that the ranch produced and turned a profit so he, Dustin, and the men who worked for them all had a good life and got the rewards their hard work merited. Sometimes that meant taking things very seriously—maybe too seriously. Growing up, his family had learned to make do with nothing. Christmases were solemn affairs because his parents often had nothing to put under the tree—if there was a tree at all that year. Marshall was determined that wasn't going to happen to his family, so he worked extra hard and was always the first one out of bed. If the early bird got the worm, then Marshall was going to make damned sure that it was him, no matter what. Responsibility sucked sometimes, but he took it seriously and he was not going to let his family down, come hell or high water.

"The Hartier house," Dusty snapped. "Apparently the estate has been settled and a young couple is moving in with two young boys." He turned away with Pal right behind him.

Marshall sighed. Dusty had been so testy lately, and Marshall had no idea what to do about it. "Really?" Marshall called. "Someone actually bought that old run-down place and is going to live there?"

Dustin paused and turned back to him. "Yeah. It's a young family. They're having it painted, and Patrick got their AC working. Anne and Richard have two young boys." He drew closer. "They were so excited about Pal, and he just soaked up all the attention." He rubbed Pal's head and stroked his back. "Didn't you? Like you're completely neglected and everyone ignores you."

For a second Marshall remembered what it was like to have those hands taking care of him. Dustin always had magic hands that could turn the coldest day into the hottest night with so little effort.

Marshall missed those days and nights. He wasn't even sure what had happened. Over twenty-five years of being together, things had changed between them. Marshall didn't know how or why any longer. They just had, and he had no idea how to get things back to the way they were. Or if it was even possible. "Well, I'm shocked. I always figured that place would need to be torn down after all those years empty. I've seen enough critters around that house for it to be infested with everything from scorpions to rattlers."

"Apparently they found a nest of a few snakes, but they've been removed. There were workmen there and a lot was happening, so they're pretty serious. I got the impression that they're from Dallas but wanted to come out here. Probably for a quieter life for the boys. Though that's just a guess." Dustin sighed. "I have a huge list of things to get done." He flashed a quick smile before heading toward the house.

Dustin was the more domestic of the two of them. Not that he wasn't an amazing rancher; he was. But Marshall was the one in charge of the cattle and managing the herd. Dustin did a lot of the inside work—though Marshall didn't think of him as "the woman" or anything. Lord, if he so much as thought such a thing, Dustin would know it and smack him up the side of the head for such Neanderthal thinking about him as well as women. Dustin was just a much better cook and he kept a clean house, which Marshall loved—so much so that he had learned over the years to not drag muddy or dusty clothes through the house. That set off Dustin like a skyrocket.

"Marshall!" Willy called as he hurried up. "We need to go. Carruthers says that he has one of our head at his place. Damned steer just wandered over there. We need to go get it and bring it back before Carruthers decides he's hungry and butchers the poor thing." His lips curled up in a smile. Old Man Carruthers was famous for winning the county fair eating contests… all of them. So the part about butchering the steer was a distinct possibility.

"Okay. Let's get going." He glanced at Dustin one more time before jumping in the truck. As usual, Marshall was in a hurry. He hated the time it took to get anywhere in trucks and cars because it was always dead time. He needed to be places, and it seemed to him that the quicker he got there, the more time he would have to get the work done. So as usual, he barreled down the road and made the turns as fast as he dared to reach the Carruthers place, then pulled the truck to a stop in a cloud of dust.

"Harry!" Marshall called as he slammed the truck door. "Thanks for calling."

"Your boy wandered into one of the pastures and just started munching like he owned the place."

Carruthers stepped out on the porch with a towel in his hands. He dried them before tossing it aside. "He was alone, so I suspect the guy is looking for the herd."

"Most likely."

"Looks like you got some real good stock. When it comes to butchering time, you call me. I'll buy one of the head off you for the freezer." Carruthers was a happy man, always ready with a quick smile, especially when it came to talking about food. He loved to eat and he loved to cook. Marshall always thought he was wasted out here. The man should have been a chef in a fancy restaurant somewhere, judging by the dishes he made for socials and things like that.

"I'll be sure to do that." Selling a few head locally was always preferable. Less transportation cost, and the local butcher could always use the business. "Now where is this guy?"

Harry pointed, and Marshall strode over. "Go bring the truck down that side road, and I'm going to get him moving." It was sometimes easier to just drive the wayward ones home than try to load the beasts into a trailer. They'd fight it anyway.

Willy signaled back, and Marshall headed out over the expanse of land, keeping an eye out for snakes and such. By the time he reached his wayward steer, he was already looking at Marshall and seemed to know that he represented the herd and home, which made things a heck of a lot easier. Marshall got him moving, and sure enough, it was easy to keep him going back toward the ranch.

By the time he got home and reunited the beast-ie with the others, Marshall was starving. Inside the house, he found a platter of sandwiches in the refrigerator all set to go, a pot of coffee on, and a plate of cut-up vegetables. Marshall huffed under his breath. They were ranchers, men who worked the land, and yet Dustin always insisted on having all this rabbit food around. He grabbed a carrot as he pulled the plates out and set them on the table while the others came in and plopped themselves into the various chairs.

"What have we got today?" Patrick asked. "The horse barn needs a good going-over, and after the fence break today, I figured Willy and I would check all the fence to make sure there aren't any more loose sections." Marshall nodded his approval. "I'll have a couple of the men clean out the barn today." He took another sandwich and ate half of it in one bite.

Marshall ate as well, his belly finally happy now that he had something in it. He munched on some of the carrots too, because they were there, and once he was finished, went out in search of Dustin.

He found him in the horse barn, already working to finish cleaning out one of the stalls. He was just starting to spread fresh bedding and had his horse saddled and in the crossties. Dustin barely looked up when he came in. "We've got one of the men who will clean this out."

"'Kay," Dustin said. He hefted a bale of straw and then another and spread them in the stall. "I appreciate that." He didn't stop his work until the stall was complete, and then he put away the tools. "I'm going out for a ride." Now that the stall was finished, he completed saddling his horse, then led him out of the barn and took off toward the east.

There had been a time when Marshall and Dustin would have ridden out together. Hell, it was something they did regularly. Now it seemed they were always going their own ways.

"Marshall, are you ready for me to get started?" Reggie asked, and Marshall nodded, pulling his attention away from Dustin. He thought about saddling up one of the horses and going after him, but there were things to be done, and the ranch needed him to see to everything and keep it running.

"Yes. That stall is done. You can clean the others and put the horses out into the pastures for the day. It will do them some good to be outside. They're calling for rain tomorrow, so make sure you bring them in again at the end of the day." He was only half paying attention, still watching as Dustin grew smaller in the distance, going farther and farther away from him.

MARSHALL WORKED the rest of the day, and once the light faded, he went inside, kicked off his boots, and headed right for the shower. He was a sweaty mess and achy as hell. But the things on his list to get completed were done, and he had met with some potential customers as well. In short, he was pretty pleased, and once clean and refreshed, he went right to his office to get a start on the books. The work on a ranch never ended, and when there wasn't something to do outside, there were always records to maintain.

"Come and eat," Dustin said from the doorway. Marshall felt him linger and then turn away before he could finish up what he was doing, leaving Marshall alone once more.

After wrapping up the last of his tasks, Marshall pushed himself out of his chair and worked the kinks from his neck and back. Getting older sucked, and his body certainly let him know it every chance it got. He stretched to work out the tightness in his legs and then left the office, following the scent of dinner to the kitchen.

Marshall sat down, and Dustin set a plate with a beautiful steak, mashed potatoes, and vegetables in front of him. Then he placed another across the table. "What do you want to drink?" Dustin asked before setting a glass of wine at his own place. Marshall hesitated, and as if he could read his mind, Dustin set down a beer for him. Then he sat down and began to eat.

Marshall turned his head down to his plate and began to eat his steak. He knew he was weird when it came to food. Marshall never liked his food mixed together, and he always ate one item and then moved on to the next. It was just the way he was, and Dustin always set his plate up so none of the food touched—unlike Dustin's plate, which was arranged artfully like something in a fancy restaurant. "How was your ride?" Marshall asked.

"Good. I checked out the fence along the road and to the east. Our patch looks good, and there were no other weak spots that direction."

Marshall lifted his gaze from his plate when Dustin paused. For a brief second, their eyes met, and Marshall's heart skipped a beat the way it had years ago.

"Don't worry, I let Patrick know so no one duplicated my work," Dustin said and returned to his dinner.

"Thanks for taking care of that," Marshall said with a sigh and ate his own meal.

"I saw the kids out playing. They waved and were so excited to see the horse." Dustin breathed heavily, and the sound drew Marshall's attention. "I don't think they've ever seen a horse up close before."

There it was—the hurt that Marshall saw in Dustin's eyes every now and then. It welled up from deep inside him and seemed to get darker every time Marshall saw it. "It was so funny how excited they were, just like with Pal." The hurt flashed away, and Dustin's lips drew upward. That smile, almost shy and gentle, was what had first drawn Marshall to Dustin. There had been something so innocent, almost boyish, about him then. Of course, Dustin had been a man when they met, a full-fledged cowboy with all the intensity and enough passion to knock Marshall off a horse and send him thudding to the arena floor... which is exactly what had happened.

Marshall held Dustin's gaze for a few seconds, and then Dustin returned to eating. Marshall did the same, finishing his perfectly juicy steak before eating the creamy potatoes. "This is good," Marshall said.

"Glad you like it," Dustin said as Marshall finished up the last. "There is some more if you want it." He got up and brought the potatoes to the table. Marshall took a little more, along with some vegetables. Dustin sat back down. "I have some running in town to do tomorrow. If there's something you need, let me know."

"Do you need me to go with you?" Marshall asked.

Dustin shrugged. "I'm just going to town. I need to pick up a new pair of boots. The ones I've got on now are wearing out. I also need some new clothes, and I thought I'd do the grocery shopping early to get it done." He barely looked up as he spoke. "Pal also needs a flea treatment."

"Okay. I'll let you know if I think of anything I need." Marshall finished his dinner and pushed back from the table and took his dishes to the sink like he always did. He then returned to his office to continue the paperwork.

The television sounded in the other room, laughter drifting into the office. Marshall got up from his desk to close the door and paused, taking a step back. Sometimes memories could be powerful, and one hit him like a bar-fight punch. A night with him and Dustin watching a movie, huddled under a blanket after the heat failed on the coldest night of the year. God, that had been so long ago. Marshall left the office and slowly made his way to the living room. Dustin sat on the sofa, his long legs spread out, with Pal curled next to him soaking up attention.

Dustin laughed at whatever he was watching, and Marshall returned to his office. The work needed to get done, and it wasn't going to finish itself. Marshall sat back down at his desk and went to work on the herd records until his eyes crossed on their own. Then he got up and turned out the lights.

As Marshall lay there looking up at the ceiling, he wondered what path had led them here. Somehow, through the years, Marshall and Dustin had taken to sleeping in separate rooms. Marshall couldn't even remember why. It wasn't as though they had had some sort of fight or anything. For some reason, what had once been their room was now his room, and Dustin slept across the hall in the old guest room. How that had happened and why was a mystery, but it had been that way for…. Marshall tried to remember that too, but he couldn't. All he knew as he closed his eyes was that he had lost something, and damned if he knew how to get it back.

Chapter 3

RANCH LIFE was always busy, and days ran together in a flurry of work and crisis resolution, the men falling into bed only to get up and do it all over again.

Then there were the differences. June in Texas meant heat, humidity, and more heat. Nothing unusual there, but waking in the night to the house rattling around him was unusual for Dustin. Rain pelted the roof, and lightning split the darkness, followed by thunder so close Dustin figured they were lucky the windows didn't shatter. Pal did something unusual—he jumped up onto the bed, shaking like a leaf.

Dustin lay still, listening and hoping the storm would pass soon. This one was a whopper, and each clap of thunder shook the house until it finally passed over.

"Dustin?" Marshall's voice called from outside, and then the door pushed open. "I think it's passing." He stepped inside in a pair of his sleep shorts.

"Is there anything else on the way?" Dustin asked, slipping out from under the covers.

"No. The line finally moved through. I'm going to go check that the buildings are intact. Stay in bed and rest. We'll probably need help with cleanup in the morning." He closed the door again and was gone.

The thunder still rolled, but it grew farther away. Dustin relaxed and climbed back into bed, his mind flashing on the time a few weeks after they'd bought the ranch when a storm like this one had come through and they'd lost the tool shed. It had completely collapsed in the wind and flying debris. After the cleanup, he and Marshall had rebuilt the shed to withstand the second coming. It had been their first big project together. Dustin smiled as he remembered the days spent working side by side.

Pal whined a little, and Dustin got back out of bed, pulled on some clothes, and let him outside. The rain was still coming down, water sluicing through the gutters and into the collection systems. He looked out across the yard, grateful the power was still on. Briefly illuminated in the floodlights, Marshall pulled the barn door closed and stomped his way out of the ring of light. Pal did his business, and then Dustin called him. He let Pal lead him around the house as he used a flashlight to check for damage. Fortunately, there didn't appear to be any, so Dustin went inside, made coffee, and got some food ready for when the guys eventually made their way inside. Then he returned to bed, Pal taking his usual place on the floor, and closed his eyes.

Dustin didn't sleep well. He dreamed of how different things were. There were times, like right now when it was quiet, that Dustin longed for a different life. When he was young, riding broncs and winning buckles and prize money, he'd dreamed of having a place of his own that he could call home. Dustin realized he had that now, but he wanted some of that excitement back… somehow.

He woke to closing doors and the guys talking. After getting up, he pulled on his clothes and found the others sitting around the table. "We were lucky," Patrick said as they all drank coffee around the packed table.

Dustin got right to work finishing breakfast. "Was it bad elsewhere?"

"A twister went through east of here. It didn't do much other than tear up some land. Folks were lucky, and we got through pretty much unscathed," Marshall explained as Dustin mixed the batter for pancakes and got the griddle good and hot. He also spread a couple pounds of bacon on baking sheets and slid them into the oven. He knew the men on their ranch, and after a night like that, they were all going to be hungry. Syrup, jam, plates, and cutlery all followed before he began flipping pancakes by the dozen.

"The farrier will be in today," Marshall explained.

"I was planning to meet him," Willy said. "I also got some repairs to do in the barn, and I want to check that roof for damage." The guys talked as Dustin got them fed. Then he sat down at his place at the end of the table with his own plate.

"Can you make some sandwiches to go?" Marshall asked.

Dustin couldn't help glaring at him. He took care of a lot around here. "I'm not a short-order cook or your mother." He glared at Marshall as chairs pushed back and the men filed out of the house as fast as they could.

"I never said you were."

"No, but you act like it. I'm the one who does your cooking. You eat, and you expect me to clean up after you all the time. I'm not your maid or your cook. I'm supposed to be your partner."

But he was starting to feel like he was just here because Marshall wanted someone to feed and pick up after him. He pushed his chair out, wishing he could pull the words back. He cleared away the dishes and left them in the sink. "I have things I need to do. If you need sandwiches to go, then you know where the stuff to make them is." He grabbed his boots and yanked them on his feet, then snagged his hat. "Come on, Pal. We got shit to do." Then he was out the back door and striding toward the truck. He wasn't sure where he was going, but he knew he needed to get away from here before he said things he couldn't take back.

He yanked the door open and climbed in after Pal, purposely not looking at the porch, because if Marshall was there, he wasn't sure he could keep his anger going. And if he wasn't, Dustin wasn't sure he could take the fact that Marshall cared so little for how he felt. So he pulled out without looking. At least that way he could still pretend.

"WHAT THE hell?" Dustin asked himself about half a mile from the ranch. Fortunately the fences were still standing, but the grass looked like it had been trampled. He continued on, drawing closer to their new neighbors. He pulled into the drive and slowed. Half the windows in the house seemed broken. Immediately, Dustin's gaze went to the roof, which seemed to be intact. Richard came out of the house carrying Oliver.

"Stay," Dustin said to Pal before getting out. "What happened? Is everyone okay?"

Richard was white as a sheet, and Oliver held him around the neck, refusing to turn around. "The storm knocked out a lot of the windows on this side the house. I think there was some hail that got driven by the wind. The inside is a mess." He rocked slowly side to side, probably to soothe Oliver.

"Where are Anne and Noah?" Dustin asked.

Richard grew even paler, if that was possible. "They're in Dallas. Noah hasn't been feeling well, and he had some tests."

Dustin thought the poor guy was going to fall over at any moment. He didn't ask what the doctors had found. That was none of his business.

"Anne is frantic about the house, and…." Okay, all this was just too much for the guy.

"All right, let's go inside," Dustin said. He pulled out his phone and made a call. "Marshall, I need your help. I'm at our new neighbors'.."

"What happened?" Marshall asked. He was clearly working and continued as he talked.

"Who do we use for glass?" Dustin asked. "These folks need some help."

"Wembley's. But I heard it's bad in a number of places," Marshall said. "It's probably going to be a while."

Dustin huffed. "Then get on the phone. Use your name, my name—hell, use any name you can think of and get someone out here to help these people. There are kids who are going to have to deal with the heat all day unless they can help." Dustin snapped at Marshall and wished he hadn't. This wasn't his fault, and he didn't understand the implications of what had happened. "Please," he added. Regardless of how things were between the two of them, Dustin didn't ask for much. Never had.

Marshall sighed. "I'll see what I can do." He hung up, and Dustin nodded.

"Okay. Let's get inside and clean things up." He led the way inside with a most likely stunned Richard behind him. The large window in the living room was intact, but the side windows had been shattered. "Where can I find a broom, dustpan, and vacuum cleaner?" Dustin asked.

Richard pointed. "In the hall closet."

"Okay. Is Oliver's room clear?" Dustin asked.

"Yes."

"Then maybe he can play in there for a little while," Dustin suggested. "If you want, I can bring Pal in to stay with you, but you have to keep him in the room with you. Okay?" Dustin asked, and Oliver actually smiled and nodded. "We don't want his paws to get cut."

"I watch him," Oliver agreed.

Dustin got Pal and carried him inside and into the bedroom with Oliver. The two immediately settled into a doggie cuddle fest as Richard closed the door.

"Okay. Let's get this glass cleaned up. At least no one will get cut." He got the broom and set Richard to work with the vacuum. They had to be thorough to get all the glass fragments.

"You don't have to do this," Richard told him, and Dustin shook his head. "I'm sure there are things to do at your place?"

"We were up in the night checking things over, and you got it worse than us." Dustin wiped down the otherwise spotless kitchen counters and then moved all the furniture before sweeping the entire floor. The glass doors remained intact, though Dustin made a note to check them over since they didn't move smoothly. Once he had the glass cleaned up, including out of the tracks for the doors, the room was at least clean and the doors operable, if still open to the outside.

Shania Twain began to play, and Dustin tugged out his phone. "Marshall?"

"I called in a longtime favor. Wembley's is on their way with a truck full of glass. They said they'd cut and replace what they needed to on-site there." Marshall still sounded annoyed.

"Thank you," Dustin told him. "This is going to mean a lot to the family. His insurance company can deal with the bill." At least the kids would have their home back. "I appreciate the help."

Marshall didn't answer right away. "You're welcome," he said softly. "We had some damage, but nothing we can't handle." He ended the call, and Dustin shoved the phone back in his pocket and went to find Richard, who had finished the living room.

"A glass company is on the way. You should call your insurance company to report the damage if you haven't already. Exactly how many windows were broken?"

"Seven," Richard answered. "And thank you. I tried calling people, but they said it would be days because their schedules were full."

"This is what neighbors are for," Dustin said. "Now let's get the rest of the house cleaned up. Once the glass is repaired, you can turn on the cooling once more and make the house comfortable."

Richard nodded, his shoulders a little straighter, and some of the near panic had left his eyes. "I'll move to our bedroom now that the living room is done. The utility room on the west corner is the worst."

"Then I'll do that next." Dustin grabbed the trash can and got to work clearing away the glass. He ended up emptying the room of cleaning materials and supplies, and some had to be thrown away because they were damaged. He kept a list for Richard, and by the time he had the glass cleaned up, workers from Wembley's had arrived. They made short work of replacing the glass, and the air conditioner hummed away before noon, cooling down the house.

"Thank you for everything," Richard said as Dustin got ready to leave. He already had his phone in hand. "I need to take this call from Anne." He answered the call, and Dustin did his best not to listen in as he went to get Pal.

Oliver sat on his little bed with Pal laid out like last week's wash. The house was cooling, but clearly the heat had had a chance to build in here. Pal's tongue lolled, and Oliver petted him like he was the center of the world. "Pal and I have to go."

Oliver lifted his gaze with those huge blue eyes of his. "Can Pal come play again? Noah will want to see him. He's really sick." How could Dustin possibly say no to that beseeching expression?

"Of course he can. And maybe someday you and Noah can come over to see the horses." When Dustin had ridden out this way a few days ago, the boys had both run to watch him riding the fence that separated the properties.

"Really?" he asked, eyes as big as saucers.

"Of course." He ruffled Oliver's hair, then roused Pal from his attention-induced coma, and they left the room. Richard was still on the phone, but from his dejected tone and pinched posture, whatever the news was, it didn't seem to be good. Dustin caught his attention, and then he and Pal left the house and headed for the truck.

Pal bounded onto the truck seat with his usual energy, and Dustin paused at the door and turned back to the house. He was worried but didn't know how to express what he felt. It would be an intrusion to ask what was happening, but his curiosity and concern were almost enough for him to find out. With a sigh, Dustin got into the truck and pulled the door closed, then started the engine. Pal settled on the bench seat next to him, head on his lap. "You liked spending time with Oliver, didn't you?"

Pal's tail thumped the seat as Dustin put the truck in Reverse and backed out of the drive. Unlike Marshall, he drove slowly. He returned to the ranch and went inside to find the breakfast dishes in the sink, along with others, probably from Marshall's foray into cooking.

Marshall was many things. He always worked hard, and he was determined—always had been. Both he and Dustin had ridden the rodeo circuit together. Dustin's event was saddle bronc, and he had been damned good. Marshall rode bulls, and as Dustin stood at the sink, loading the dishwasher, he remembered Marshall on a bull—the power, the finesse. The first time he'd set eyes on Marshall had been at a rodeo in Albuquerque. Dustin had won his event, and he stood at the rails as the gate burst open. For eight seconds, the world seemed to stop and all that mattered was Marshall on that bull, man against beast—and in this case, the stunning man came out on top. At least until the bull chased Marshall right into the wall in front of him. By the time Dustin had the kitchen cleaned up, his daydream had come to an end and reality once again pushed its way back to center stage.

"How did it work out at the neighbors'?" Marshall asked.

"The glass company has come and gone. Thank you for that." He bit his lower lip. "There's something going on over there. Richard and the older son were home. I brought Pal in so he could play with Oliver while I helped clean up, and Oliver told me that Noah is really sick. Richard said something about tests, but apparently they didn't come back well." He sighed and turned back to wiping out the sink.

"You know that isn't your business," Marshall said.

"I never said it was," Dustin snapped.

"Then why are you getting so worked up you're going to scrub through the bottom of the sink?" Marshall had his arms crossed over his chest in that definitive way he had when Dustin whirled around. Sometimes that look—sort of smoldering in a strong way—could turn him on faster than a Texas twister. It was pure cocky cowboy, and that was Marshall to a tee. And yet right now, all he wanted to do was smack that look off his face.

"How can I not be a little worried? He's a boy about four years old, and Richard seemed worried out of his mind." He groaned again. "I know it's none of my business what's going on, and I'm not going to gossip or snoop. But I want to try to help. It's the neighborly thing to do."

Marshall shook his head. "Look. I know you have a huge heart. Always have. But we have our own problems and worries here. Maybe if…."

Dustin dropped the scrubbie in the sink. "Are we in trouble?" As soon as the words were out of his mouth, he realized that question could have many different meanings, because it seemed to him that he and Marshall *were* in trouble—at least in some ways. "Is there something I need to know? Is business bad?"

"No. We're doing very well. The herd is growing, and we're selling all of the beef we can raise. Our quality is top of the scale, and we get the most we can for each head."

"Okay." He put his hands on his hips. "Do I not pull my weight? Am I ever not there when you need me?" Dustin scowled slightly. "I work a hell of a lot around here, and I don't get any credit for it. I feed you and I take care of all the men and you know it. You'd be up to your armpits in God knows what if it weren't for me, so don't go insinuating shit." He stared daggers at his partner.

Marshall actually took a step back. "That's not my point. You and I have worked hard for years to make this ranch a success. Our ranch is respected, and we get top dollar for our beef because of all of our hard work." He stepped closer. "Do you remember how hard it was when we started out? Half the people in town wouldn't talk to us. Remember that time that the sheriff showed up because he got wind that some folks were going to teach the fags a lesson?"

"So? Being neighborly and helping others doesn't change any of that. In fact, it may mean that we have friends, and you help folks out so that when you need it, they'll help you." Dustin sighed and figured what the hell. Sometimes talking to Marshall was like kicking a brick wall. You got nowhere, and in the end your feet hurt. "I'm here now. Is there something you need me to do?" The house was spotless, and he had been about to head out to see what needed to be done in the barns.

"I guess I...." Marshall rubbed the back of his neck before turning and leaving the house. There were times that even after all these years, Dustin wondered if he was ever going to be able to figure Marshall out. It was funny how things that used to bind them together now seemed to just get on his nerves.

Chapter 4

"I'M GOING to start you in here," Marshall told Jackson a week later, showing him around the horse barn. Jackson had turned up because some of Marshall's old rodeo buddies had thought he might be hiring. He had apparently taken one too many rides on the bulls and was never going to be able to ride again. The guys had pointed Jackson his way, and Marshall needed another hand, so he decided to give the kid a shot. "I need all the stalls cleared out and new bedding put down. There's hay in the loft, and you know where the water is. I expect the barn to be kept clean at all times. Once the stalls are done, you can check out the tack room, make sure that's organized and everything is put away."

"Sure, Marshall. I will, and thank you." Jackson seemed like he'd lost his confidence with that last fall. Marshall knew what that felt like and how hard it was to try to start over without the one thing in life you thought you were good at. Hell, Marshall had started over more times in his life than he could remember. His home life had been awful, with a

stepfather who loved his whiskey and was the mean-
est drunk Marshall had ever encountered. After he'd
left at sixteen, he'd had to start over to figure out
how to feed himself. Then the carnival for a year,
the rodeo, building a life with Dustin, and finally the
ranch. Change was hard, and each time it required a
leap of faith—something he wasn't so sure he had
anymore.

"You don't need to thank me. I believe in paying my people well, but I expect a lot from them.
Ask Patrick or Willy if you have any questions. They
both know the ropes really well." Marshall scowled
as he noticed Jackson's attention wander and then
snap back to where it should be. "Get yourself to
work. There will be sandwiches and things in the
house for lunch."

Marshall left the barn and made a mental note
to check back in a few hours. There was no reason
Jackson couldn't fit in on the ranch if he wanted to.
According to Marshall's buddy Wilton, Jackson had
grown up on a ranch, but things hadn't worked out
so well for him.

"Marshall," Dustin said as he strode into the
barn.

Marshall turned, but not before he noticed the
way Jackson's attention focused. He would have
growled at the guy, but Dustin seemed… different
somehow. *Off.* "What is it?" he asked, heading out
of the barn, guiding Dustin along with him as he
made his way to the equipment shed. Marshall liked
to check the herd on horseback, but his nose told him

another bout of rain was likely on the way, and using a four-wheeler would be faster.

"I know you…." He sighed.

"Just say it," Marshall said.

"I got back from doing the grocery shopping, and you know the people at the store. It's like information central. Those people seem to know everything about everyone else long before they know it themselves. Anyway… I know how you feel, but…."

"Stop beating around that bush. Soon there isn't going to be anything left." Marshall tried to smile. "Just tell me what it is and I'll try to fix it."

Dustin's expression darkened. "This isn't something you can fix… or any of us can." He bit his lower lip until Marshall wondered if it was going to bleed. "It's Noah."

"The new neighbor's kid?" Marshall asked. It wasn't like he was heartless, but it was all he could manage to keep the ranch going and his family's heads above water. Everyone on the ranch depended on them to provide, and Marshall didn't have a lot of extra energy for anything else. Sometimes he hated that he wasn't twenty any longer and couldn't do everything for everyone. "What about him?"

"He has leukemia," he whispered, the same way Dustin's mother used to when she talked about someone's illness. Marshall always wondered about that phenomenon. Like saying the name of the disease was bad, and if God heard you say it, then he'd give it to you too. "Marshall, he's four years old and he has cancer."

"Is he in the hospital?" Marshall asked.

Dustin shook his head. "He's home for now. But Anne and Noah are making regular trips to the hospital. I can't help feeling for them and what they're going through." His big heart had always been one of Dustin's biggest attractions. In the ring, Dustin had been a force to be reckoned with. He went after what he wanted with everything he had. But outside of the arena, Marshall had come to learn that Dustin had a real heart that had been battered and bruised more than he ever wanted to say. It had taken Marshall months to learn that Dustin had lost his little sister to childhood leukemia. Though for Dustin, it had been the revelations of the people who should have loved him that had caused the most heartache. Not that it mattered. Your family turning their back on you, no matter the reason, left a scar. "I need to get to work and try to take my mind off it." Dustin strode away with his long legs toward one of the other buildings.

Marshall frowned to find Jackson watching, and then went back to work. He had his own growing list of things to do. He headed to the equipment shed, jumped on an ATV, and zoomed out to get the work done. He repaired another weak spot in the fence and looked toward the west, where clouds were building. Marshall jumped back on the ATV once he'd finished the section of fence, and headed over to check on the herd, which was just over a slight rise.

He watched the animals as they slowly moved through the field, munching their grass. Ranching was a funny business. It had a lot of the same risks as any living made so close to the land. But sitting on the ATV, watching the cattle as they moved in their quiet way, soothed him. Not much else did now, and lately Marshall was beginning to wonder just what his life had become.

The sun disappeared behind the clouds, and Marshall lifted his hat and wiped his brow with the back of his hand. Thankfully, this bout of weather didn't look anywhere near as strong as the last one. He started the engine of the ATV and headed back toward the ranch house as the first rumbles of thunder rolled over the land.

Marshall made it back just as the rain began. He put the ATV away and made a break for the house as the rain pelted the ground. Inside, Marshall took off his boots. "Where is everyone?" he asked Dustin. The table held the remnants of lunch.

"They ate and rushed out to beat the rain." Dustin pulled a pot off the stove and set it aside.

"What are you doing?" Marshall asked, inhaling the amazing scent. "Is that for dinner?"

Dustin shook his head. "No. I'm making baked penne to take to the neighbors," he explained. "They're trying to help their children, and I thought they could use a meal that they didn't have to cook." He continued what he was doing, and Marshall turned toward the living room to check on the weather since he'd have to wait out the rain before he could get back to work. Instead, Marshall paused. In that moment, if someone were to ask him why he did it, he wouldn't be able to give an answer, but he did.

"Do you need some help?" Marshall asked, approaching Dustin, who smiled. For a second Dustin looked every bit the cocky kid he'd been after he'd just won one of the many buckles in the display case in the living room corner. "That stuff is the best."

Dustin chuckled, a warm, almost joyous sound. "You really want to help?" he asked. "Then you can drain the pasta for me. I don't want it to cook too much." He moved to another area of the kitchen.

Marshall used a colander to drain away the water. "You know, we could bake something for the kids. Do you have any cookie recipes?" he asked.

The smile he got from Dustin grew even brighter. "You know I do." He opened a drawer and pulled out a book. "What do you think of these? Good old-fashioned chocolate chip."

Marshall nodded as he looked over the recipe. Those were his favorite, though they hadn't had them in a while.

"I'll finish up the pasta. Why don't you get the ingredients together for the cookies?"

Marshall agreed and began looking for what he needed. Dustin seemed amused by his searching, and more than once Marshall found himself bumping against Dustin. It was strange—they had been together for many years, and he couldn't remember the last time they had worked together like this. It must have been during those early years when the two of them had had nothing, and yet they'd been happy doing everything together.

"The flour is in those canisters. Sugar too. You'll need the brown sugar from the pantry," Dustin told him with another of those smiles that made his heart beat faster. "Don't spill the flour everywhere," he warned.

Marshall took a pinch and blew it in Dustin's direction.

"You don't want to start something you can't finish," Dustin chuckled.

"Okay. How is the pasta coming?" Marshall teased.

Dustin got the dish in the lower of the two ovens. "All set. Now it just needs to bake." He got a bowl and handed it to Marshall, who read the recipe and began mixing ingredients. This was fun and tasty as he snagged a few fingerfuls of dough. "Stop that," Dustin chided as Marshall licked his fingers dramatically, playing with Dustin a little. "Go ahead and add the chips."

"Okay." He loved chocolate chips and snuck a few.

Dustin got out the cookie sheets, and once they had mixed the dough, they used spoons to parcel out dollops before sliding the sheets into the oven. "Now we wait until they're done. Of course, you could help me clean up."

Marshall checked out the window. It was still raining. Marshall tried to remember the last time he had wished for it not to stop. Rain always meant that most work stopped. Some tasks needed to be done inside, and light rain rarely halted what needed to be done outdoors. But this time of year, when the rain came, it usually meant short, torrential bursts.

"You want me to load the dishwasher?" Marshall asked.

"Sure. You remember playing Tetris on that old game in the arena in Boise? Well, think of it as Tetris with dishes." Dustin was clearly enjoying this, and his mirth increased as Marshall apparently loaded the dishes the wrong way. "Like this." He took Marshall's hand, his touch strong yet gentle. "Put them this way."

It was stupid to feel attracted like this while leaning over the dishwasher, but in that split second, Marshall realized how much he'd missed Dustin.

But that was stupid too, and he shook it off. Dustin was right here. They lived in the same house and they saw each other all the time. Maybe Marshall was going crazy. He'd heard that happened as people got older, and he was going to turn fifty in a few years. Maybe senility was catching up with him. "Dustin… I…." *Damn.* He swallowed hard and licked his lips.

Dustin pulled his hand back. "Yeah, I know. You can figure it out."

Marshall straightened up. "I didn't mean it that way." His voice rumbled in this throat. "I suck at this sort of stuff, so thanks for showing me." He met Dustin's gaze and nearly lost himself in those deep, open-sky blue eyes and lips that he remembered having a hint of peppermint from the Tic Tacs he was always sucking on. "Look, Dustin, I know things…." He found himself leaning in, the old attraction flaring to life once more.

"Marshall! Frenzy jumped his corral during the storm!" Patrick called from the back door.

Marshall turned toward the voice, tamping down his frustration at the interruption. "I'll be right there." He switched his attention back to Dustin. "I need to go, but baking with you was fun." He was about to say something ridiculous like they needed to do it again, but it sounded stupid in his head.

"You have to go," Dustin told him, and Marshall headed for the back door and pulled on his boots. He turned to tell Dustin that he'd be back as soon as he could, but Dustin was already back to work, finishing up in the kitchen, and Marshall had a horse to find before something happened to him.

"How many times have I told you not to leave him out?"

"Jackson didn't know," Patrick answered, and Marshall growled at himself. Of course the guy who just started didn't know that Frenzy was a jumper. If his temperament had been different, he might have made a great dressage horse or even a steeplechaser. But instead he was a ranch horse who loved to jump any corral he was put in, especially during storms, when he tended to spook.

"Well, let's go find him. Saddle up our horses and we'll get going. If we take the ATVs, he'll only run from us more." Patrick hurried away, and Marshall did a quick check of the various buildings to make sure everything was sound. Then he joined Patrick with the horses, and they rode out.

"Did I interrupt something with you and Dustin?" Patrick asked once they finally picked up some sign of Frenzy. "You know we could have gone out to find a horse without you."

Marshall swallowed. "He and I were—"

"Then you should have told me to bug off," Patrick interrupted.

"We were cooking and baking cookies for the neighbor's kids," Marshall clarified, even as his cheeks heated. "In fact, you did me a favor, because I didn't have to finish loading the dishwasher." He tried to cover his discomfort.

Marshall pulled to a stop as Frenzy came into view. "There he is." They slowed and approached cautiously. Frenzy stood at the edge of one of the pastures near a line of old, gnarled trees. Thankfully, he didn't give them any trouble, and Marshall was easily able to lead him back to the ranch and get him in his stall.

"You want a brushing?" Marshall asked the horse. He often talked to them as he worked. He left the stall and got the combs and brushes before returning and closing the door. Marshall always loved working with the horses, and he fell into a familiar rhythm as he worked.

"I think you're crazy. Dustin is hot," Jackson said to the squeak of the old wheelbarrow wheel. The words pulled Marshall out of his thoughts, and he ground his teeth.

"You get that notion out of your head right quick," Willy snapped. "Dustin's hotness is none of your concern. He's Marshall's partner, and those two have been together for twenty-odd years." The words were punctuated with the scrape of metal on concrete.

"I know," Jackson said. "But that doesn't change the fact that Dustin is still super hot. Looking is free."

"Not if Marshall catches you. It might cost you two front teeth and a job. Now talk less and get this work done before Marshall hears you jawing like that," Willy growled.

Marshall went back to grooming Frenzy. It seemed Willy was going to put the kid in his place and Marshall didn't have to do a thing about it… at least for now. But Jackson did get Marshall thinking. Dustin *was* hot, and he'd always been sexy as hell. So what the heck had happened between them? Maybe it was Marshall, and Dustin just wasn't interested anymore.

Marshall finished up with the horse and left the stall. He put away the brushes and combs and then strode out of the barn, making sure Jackson saw him. But Marshall didn't say a word. Let the kid wonder if Marshall had heard him. Dustin was his, and Marshall would be damned if some kid was going to swoop in to make a play for him.

Chapter 5

THERE WERE so many times that Dustin knew what Marshall was going to do before he did it. But having him help in the kitchen was not one of those times. And then Marshall started acting weird, and once again Dustin wondered what his partner was thinking. He sighed as he pulled the tin out of the cupboard and filled it with some of the cooled cookies. He set the tin on the table and pulled the glass dish from the oven, set the lid on it, and slid it into the insulated carrying container.

"Hey. Did you forget something?" Dustin asked as Marshall paused in the doorway. "I'm going to head over to the neighbors'."

"I thought I'd go with you," Marshall said. Dustin thought he could have been knocked over with a feather. "That is, if you want me to."

"Sure." He shrugged, wondering at this sudden interest. Still, he wasn't going to complain. He and Marshall had been on separate paths for long enough that Dustin figured that there was little hope of those paths coming back together. Of course, this could be just one of those twists and turns that were part of the journey, but he'd take it for what it was. "But I'm driving." He flashed Marshall a smile and was surprised to see one in return. "Come on, Pal. Going for a ride."

Pal raced past them and was sniffing at the truck door when they got there. Dustin waited for Marshall to get in before handing him the dish and the tin. He let Pal jump into the truck, then got in and started the engine and carefully pulled out of the drive, heading to the neighbors' place.

"Daddy, it's Mr. Dustin," Oliver called. "Mommy!"

Richard joined Oliver on the porch as Dustin and Marshall got out of the truck. Pal hurried over to say hello to his friend and was instantly in doggie heaven at the attention.

"We didn't mean to intrude," Dustin said, "but we made some cookies, and I brought some home-made pasta for dinner. I figured that with all the activity, you might need a break."

"That's so kind," Richard said. "Come on in. Oliver, you can play with Pal out here, but stay close to the house."

"I will, Daddy," Oliver answered, already sitting with Pal on the grass as Richard led the way inside.

Anne sat in one of the heavily used living room chairs with Noah on her lap. He seemed half asleep and pale. "Thank you," Anne said after Richard explained what they brought.

"You're welcome." Dustin smiled. "I don't believe you've met Marshall, my partner. Marshall, this is Richard and Anne, and the sleepy one is Noah."

"Thank you both for coming," Anne said. "Mostly I want to thank you for bringing Pal. Oliver has been asking when he could visit him again." She seemed drawn and almost as tired as the boy in her arms. "Please sit down. I think we have some coffee somewhere. Let me just put him in bed for a while." Anne slowly got up and left the room. She returned a few minutes later and half slumped into the chair.

"Is there anything we can do?" Dustin asked.

Anne shook her head, and Richard sat in the chair closest to her. "The doctors said that with the start of treatment, he was going to be tired all the time." The two of them had the same haunted look in their eyes.

"I'm going to the treatments with Noah, and Richard is staying here so Oliver can have as normal a life as possible." She leaned forward as the scent of coffee wafted into the room. Richard jumped up and returned with a tray of mugs and a few crackers on a tray, which he set on the coffee table.

"Thanks for bringing Pal over. Oliver loves him, and he needs someone to brighten his day." As if called, Oliver came inside with Pal right behind him. He stopped, looking at Marshall, his eyes wide and his mouth hanging open.

"Are you one of the cowboys on the horsey?" he asked. Oliver must have been too enthralled with Pal to have noticed Marshall before.

"Yes. You might have seen me on my horse. His name is Custer, and he's a really good horse."

Oliver nodded, the expression of complete awe not diminishing a single iota. "You're a real cowboy with a lasso and everything?" He stepped closer as though Marshall was the most fascinating person on earth.

"I haven't lassoed anything in a while. But yes, I'm a cowboy, and so is Dustin. Before we bought the ranch, he rode broncs in the rodeo, and I rode bulls." Marshall leaned forward so he was speaking directly to Oliver. Dustin wished he had a camera. Marshall had never related particularly well to children before.

"Did you win?" Oliver asked.

"We both did. When you win in the rodeo, you get a belt buckle." Marshall removed his belt and handed it to Oliver. "This is one I won here in Texas. I was state champion one year, and that's why it has the state and a longhorn on it. I like this one best because it's from here in Texas. Dustin has one like it too, and he has a world championship buckle too. I never got one of those. I came second one year, through."

Oliver ran his fingers over the embossing. "Mama, they're *real* cowboys," he told her. "Maybe I can be a cowboy when I grow up."

Marshall ruffled Oliver's hair, looking at Richard and Anne for guidance. Richard smiled slightly, and Anne seemed a little lost, but didn't balk at the idea. "You can be anything you want to be. Maybe someday I'll show you some cowboy stuff. Can you ride a horse?" Oliver shook his head. "Then that's the first thing you have to learn, if your mom and dad think it's okay. Real cowboys ride horses some of the time."

"Daddy," Oliver said, pooching out his lower lip. That had to be a well-practiced move, Dustin was pretty sure. "Can I get a horse so I can be a cowboy?"

"Taking care of a horse is a big responsibility. You have to feed him, water him, clean up after him, and make sure that he's cared for, and then you have to ride him and love him lots," Marshall said. "You know, maybe a horse is something you can get when you're older."

Oliver didn't miss a beat. "Then how can I be a cowboy?" He put his hands on his hips, and Dustin grinned.

"He's got you there," Dustin teased. "Maybe you can visit the horses someday, okay?" he offered. That seemed to satisfy Oliver, and his parents both nodded.

Oliver was happy and climbed onto the sofa next to his dad, but he continued looking at Marshall like he hung the moon.

"Oliver, why don't you take Pal out to play?" Anne asked. Oliver sighed dramatically and then slid off the sofa.

"Go play," Dustin told Pal, and he bounded outside after Oliver, the screen door banging closed after them. Richard closed the inside door to save the bought air and then sat back down.

"He loves animals. Every time he sees one of you on the property nearby, Oliver stands at the window to watch," Richard told both of them.

Dustin leaned forward. "How is Noah doing?" he asked quietly.

Anne sighed softly and then shrugged. "It's hard to tell. The therapy is so hard on him, and we stay in Dallas. Then once he's a little stronger, he can come home for a while, only to have to go back for the next treatment." She bit her lower lip as the scent of the pasta wafted into the room.

"Do you want some of the pasta?" Richard asked both of them. "It smells amazing. Anne is an incredible cook, but she's been so busy."

"Please go ahead. We're fine. I made a separate dish for us and the guys," Dustin lied, but he didn't want them to feel obligated to feed them. "Please eat while it's hot."

Richard returned with two plates and handed one to Anne, who ate ravenously. Dustin glanced at Marshall and found him looking back. *You were right*, he mouthed, and Dustin nearly fell out of his chair. Marshall was many things—strong, opinionated, and hardworking—but he was also prideful, so that had to have been hard for him to admit.

"This is so good," Richard moaned around his bite.

"We've been so busy trying to keep all the balls in the air with Noah and getting Oliver ready for school, the new house, and Richard working from home and trying to care for Oliver," Anne explained. "It's hard to be apart, especially when there are important decisions to make for both of us and the other isn't there." She took Richard's hand. "His support means everything." She squeezed his fingers and then released his hand so she could return to eating.

"Marshall and I don't mean to take up your time," Dustin began as he stood to go. "But like we said earlier, if you need anything or if there's something we can do, just let us know. Oh, and be sure that Noah gets some of the cookies." He smiled, and Anne nodded while Richard saw them to the door.

"Thank you," he said softly, his voice rough. "We appreciate all the help."

Dustin opened the door, and he and Marshall stepped outside into the early evening air. Oliver and Pal were playing get the stick, with Pal having a ball.

"Oliver, come on in and wash up to eat," Richard called. "Pal needs to go home now."

"Awww," he said as he came over.

Dustin called Pal, and after saying goodbye, he and Marshall got in the truck and headed for home. Dustin somehow managed to make it back to the ranch, park, and turn off the engine before his eyes filled. He wiped them, damned determined that neither Marshall nor anyone else was going to see him cry. But he wasn't fast enough, and before Dustin could open his door, Marshall pulled him into a hug. He didn't say anything, just held him and sat in the warming cab. Then, after a few seconds, he let him go, got out, and stomped across the yard toward the barn, calling out to the men that there was still plenty to do.

DUSTIN PULLED a dish of pasta out of the oven and set it on the table. He figured since he'd made a batch of his baked penne earlier, he'd make a second. He was hungry for it now, and by the time it was done, Marshall and some of the guys had come in. This was a great eat-on-the-go type dish, and on a ranch, everyone was always on the go.

"How is Jackson working out?" Marshall asked Patrick.

"If he pays more attention to his work and gets his head out of the clouds, he'll be just fine. I'll keep an eye on him for a while. His work is good, and he isn't sloppy, so that's a good thing. But he doesn't seem to be thinking with his big head." The others around the table nodded and chuckled.

"I think he's used to being the center of attention and getting whatever he wants. I checked his standings, and he was doing really well on the rodeo circuit before he got hurt the last time." Marshall turned his attention to Dustin. "You remember what being at the top of the game was like. Everyone wanted your attention, and they wanted to be you or be with you, if you know what I mean."

"Yeah," Dustin agreed. "But I seem to remember that there was only one person whose attention I really wanted." He met Marshall's gaze across the table and watched him swallow as the heat in the room kicked up a few degrees. "I guess I was lucky that I knew what I wanted, and by that time I had figured out what was really important and worth going after." At least it had been worth it at the time. Not that he and Marshall had had a bad life together in any way. Things had just changed so much over the past twenty-some years. The heart-pounding feeling and the passion seemed to have slipped away, and as he sat at the opposite end of the table from his partner, he felt like he had grown so distant from the most important person in his life that the table looked to grow longer and longer with each passing meal.

For a second, as he watched Marshall, their gazes caught. Dustin tilted his head in confusion. He thought he might have seen his own sadness and longing reflected back at him, but it flashed away in mere seconds when one of the guys asked Marshall a question. After that, he was engrossed in a conversation about their plans for later in the year when things dried out, and where they were going to move the herds so they could be closer to the long-term sources of water.

This part of Texas was not nearly as dry as the west side of the state, but it had periods when rain could be scarce, so it was always best to have a plan for those times. Fortunately, one of the beauties of their land was a permanent water supply that ran through the northern edge of the property. Even in the driest years, the stream never dried up. It was fed by a spring some ten miles away, but it ran faithfully no matter what. It was also part of their deed that they could build a retention pond, which they had done years ago, and that gave them another source of water, but the pond could dry up, whereas the creek never did.

At the end of dinner, the guys all took care of their dishes and thanked him before leaving the house. Dustin was antsy and wanted to talk to Marshall, but he went out with the men, leaving Dustin alone. Refusing to stay inside any longer, Dustin went to the barn to saddle his horse and go for a ride to try to clear his head.

"Hi, Dustin." A man flashed him a hundred-watt smile as he extended his hand after yanking off his glove. "I'm Jackson."

"It's good to meet you," Dustin said, shaking the man's hand. "I understand you just started."

There was that smile again. "Yes. A friend heard you were looking for help, and I'm grateful for the work. I rode rodeo the way you and Marshall did, though I never had your success. The injuries caught up with me, and I can't do that any longer. Though I did make it to the finals one year, and they played highlights of the world champion rides. I got to see you on Tornado. That was something else." His eyes sparkled with excitement. "I always wondered what it would be like to be able to ride like you."

"That was a long time ago," Dustin said. "But thanks." He turned away to get his horse, but felt Jackson's gaze on him. He decided to ignore it and get going. If he acknowledged Jackson's interest in any way, he'd be encouraging it. Though it was sort of flattering to know that a young guy like Jackson found him attractive. In a way, he liked it. Not that he had any intention of doing anything about it. But still….

"Jackson, don't you have things to do besides standing around?" Marshall snapped. "Get finished up if you want to continue working here." He turned and left the barn like the whirlwind he could be, and Dustin got his horse in the crossties, saddled him,

and then led him outside. Marshall was nowhere to
be seen, so he urged Whistler forward and out toward the retention pond.

Time in the saddle gave him a chance to think,
which could be good and bad. Maybe he was becoming existential in his middle age, but he kept wondering if there wasn't more than what he had. Dustin
knew he should be grateful. He and Marshall had a
ranch of their own, and they didn't fight, though he
wondered if maybe it wouldn't be better if they did
sometimes. At least he'd know that Marshall cared
about something other than the ranch and being out
with the cattle.

The sun shone off the water as he approached,
and Dustin slipped off the horse and let him munch,
holding the reins as he stood near the edge of the small
body of water. In the distance he could see Anne and
Richard's house. Dustin wondered if Oliver could see
him, and he waved broadly just in case.

Damn, he had just about everything he had ever
dreamed about. He had a family, a home, a place
where he belonged, and people who would fight if
any of those were threatened. But in all his dreams,
Dustin never pictured his life devoid of passion or
himself as part of a family of just two. When he'd
been young, his view of family had been set by the
images he saw. And they had stayed with him. Marshall used to tell him he was naïve, and maybe he
had been to think that they could have children like
everyone else. It had been one of the areas where he
and Marshall had disagreed, but Dustin had backed
away because he loved Marshall. Hell, he still did,

but if someone didn't want to be a father, it wasn't fair to foist it on them.

Dustin sighed, still watching the sun as it shimmered across the surface of the mostly still water. At least it looked that way on the surface. The beauty of their pond was that they had designed it to overflow back into the stream so that at times of high water, there was water movement to help keep it fresh. There had been times when he and Marshall would come down here and take a swim in the evening. More than once the two of them had waded in after stripping off their clothes and ended up making love in the water. Unfortunately it had been quite a while since they had done something like that, and it didn't look like that portion of their lives was going to come back any time soon. Yeah, he was getting older, but maybe the time had come to make a decision about what he wanted the rest of his life to look like.

Chapter 6

MARSHALL WAS exhausted. Everything that could go wrong certainly seemed to have completely fallen apart in the last few days. Just today, Willy had trouble with one of the ATVs, and then Patrick backed his truck into one of the fence posts, which had to be repaired immediately before the herd found it. A small group of cattle got mired in some mud, and Marshall had to pull them out, which resulted in mud up to his hips and his jeans squishing until he could get back to the house for a change of clothes and a shower.

At least that had been the plan, until Jackson reported that Frenzy was kicking at his stall and wouldn't calm down for anyone. To top it off, Marshall caught Jackson watching Dustin like he was some sort of buffet again. If that didn't stop, the kid was going to find himself punched into next week and sent packing.

It was dark by the time Marshall had calmed the horse and gotten all of the fires put out for the day. By then his jeans had dried to a caked-on mess and he was wondering if he was going to have to cut them off. Needless to say, he was in a mood and at the very end of his patience.

"What happened to you?" Dustin said as soon as Marshall walked in the door.

"Just don't start." He didn't even want to talk about it.

"Take off those pants and boots and leave them in the mud room," Dustin told him. "I'll take care of them. Then get a quick shower and have some dinner. Richard and Anne have to make an emergency run to Dallas with Noah, so they're going to bring Oliver here overnight. Richard will pick him up tomorrow about noon."

Marshall cleared his throat. He wanted to object, but he didn't have the energy. "I'm…." He swallowed his words and peeled off his jeans. "I take it they will be here any minute." All he wanted to do was eat, maybe sit for a while, and then go to bed. Of course he also had work to do in the office because the damned paperwork never fucking ended.

"Probably five minutes," Dustin told him, and Marshall got his boots and his jeans off before trudging to the bathroom in his muddy boxers.

The skin on his legs ached from where the mud and dirt had rubbed, and the water ran brown when he stepped under it. He rested against the tile and just let the water fall over him, hoping it would make him feel human again and not like some growly bear, because Oliver didn't need to hear him grumping and whining. After the few days he'd had, a visitor in the form of a seven-year-old was the last thing he needed.

Marshall turned off the water and stepped out of the shower, then toweled off before going to his room, where he dressed in light clothes before following voices to the kitchen.

Oliver sat at the table with a bowl of ice cream and a cookie. "Do you promise?" he asked.

"Yes. Your papa will be back in the morning. But they had to take Noah to the hospital right away. It will be fun here. Pal will probably sleep near your bed and everything." Dustin smiled, and the worried look slipped from Oliver's face. Dustin always seemed to know what to say to make things better.

"Where's your cowboy hat?" Oliver asked as Marshall sat down.

"It's not right to wear your hat in the house. I hung it up by the back door when I came in from outside."

"Dinner will be ready for you in a few minutes," Dustin told him, and Marshall got an idea. He stood, left the room, and went to his closet. It took him a few minutes to find the old box that had been his as a kid, resting on the top shelf. He took the box to the table and sat back down.

"When I was your age, I got this." He pulled the old, beat-up hat out of the box. "It was my first cowboy hat." Marshall hadn't thought of it in years, but his father had given it to him. Marshall set it on Oliver's head. "There you go. Now you can be a cowboy just like Dustin and me."

Oliver grinned and then set the hat on the next chair. "Cowboys don't wear their hats in the house."

That was so cute. Marshall wished his men listened to him like that.

Dustin set his plate in front of him and then kissed the top of his head before moving away. Marshall turned, wondering what that was for. He followed Dustin with his gaze, wishing for more of those. Hell, as Dustin busied himself in the kitchen, Marshall was tempted to get up, wind his arms around him, and find out if Dustin's lips were as sweet as they always had been. Maybe once Oliver was in bed, he could join Dustin, and maybe he'd find out. That thought raced through his mind, lighting a fire he thought had largely gone out.

"Mr. Marshall, can I see the horses?" Oliver asked, pulling Marshall's attention.

"Marshall is tired, so how about I take you out to see the horses?" Dustin offered, and Oliver's lower lip quivered.

"But he's the cowboy," Oliver said.

Marshall sighed. "Oliver, Mr. Dustin is a bigger cowboy than me." He stood and held out his hand. Oliver took it, and Marshall led him into the living room. "See?" He led Oliver over to the case in the corner and turned on the light. "Those are all the rodeo belt buckles that Dustin and I won. You see that biggest one? The one at the very top? That one is Mr. Dustin's. He won it when he was world champion. The best there was."

Oliver's eyes widened and his mouth hung open. "But he doesn't look like a cowboy, like you."

"Well, being a cowboy is in here." He touched Oliver's heart. "It's all about who you are and not so much about how you look. See, a cowboy is a lot of things. He's honest, hardworking, and he always stands up for the people he loves."

"Like Mommy, Daddy, and Noah?" Oliver asked.

"Yes. Just like that. See, you staying here so they can take Noah to the hospital is a cowboy thing to do. You're helping your family by being a big boy so they can be with Noah." Marshall watched as Oliver's little shoulders squared. "See, just like that." Marshall took Oliver's hand once more and led him back to the table. "Finish your ice cream, and then both of us will take you to see the horses."

Oliver nodded and ate. Marshall finished his dinner as Dustin settled his hands on Marshall's shoulders. He just left them there, and Marshall wondered what was going on when he got another of those kisses on the head, and then Dustin moved away. He finished his dinner and took care of his own dishes. "Ready to see the horses? Don't forget your hat."

Oliver put it on, and Marshall took his hand, with Dustin taking the other, and they crossed the yard to the horse barn. Marshall pushed open the door and turned on the lights. "These are all the horses we use on the ranch.

"Were any of the horseys in the rodeo too?" Oliver asked.

"No. These are working horses. Rodeo horses are bred especially for that. But these are the kind you can ride." Marshall lifted Oliver so he could see into the stalls.

"Here. Custer is a real nice horse. He's the one Mr. Marshall rides. You can give him a carrot if you want." Dustin handed him one. "Put it flat on your palm. He has big teeth, but he won't use them."

Oliver was so cute as he held out his hand, and he giggled as Custer took the carrot. That horse was the gentlest eater Marshall had ever seen, and Oliver had a ball feeding him carrots. "There are other ones too." He set Oliver down and led him through the barn, introducing him to each of the horses. "This one is Frenzy. He likes to jump." Actually, he was too wild for what they needed, and Marshall was considering selling him, but he didn't need to tell Oliver that.

"Nice horsey," Oliver said, giggling as Frenzy blew his breath out. "He sneezed."

"He was just breathing hard at you. Horses snort sometimes," Dustin said, patting Frenzy's nose. Then they moved on so Oliver could see each of the horses in the barn. "There used to be more horses on the ranch, but now we have four-wheelers too. So we don't need as many horses, but it's hard to be a cowboy without a horse."

Oliver turned to him and then back to Dustin. "You're a cowboy in here." He put his hand on his chest, and Marshall couldn't help it. He grinned and hugged Oliver.

"That's right." He set Oliver down. "Cowboys also get up pretty early in the morning, so we should go back inside and get ready for bed." He held

Oliver's hand and led him across the yard and into the house. "Can you get cleaned up and then put your jammies on?" Marshall asked, and Oliver nodded, the hat nearly falling off as he did. Then he hurried down the hall, and Marshall watched him go. "He's something else."

Dustin nodded, an expression of sheer longing on his face, and Marshall knew he had been the one to put it there. It had been his decision not to have children, though Dustin had agreed to it. But the wishing he saw in Dustin's eyes sent a pang of regret through him. Maybe that was why the two of them had grown apart? That at least had to be part of it. "You're so good with him." Dustin's gaze didn't shift, but Marshall felt a change anyway. "I heard you in the living room, the way you talked to Oliver about what a cowboy is, and you showed him my buckle." He wandered over to the sink and started loading the dishwasher. "I haven't felt like a cowboy in a very long time."

"Mr. Marshall?" Oliver said as he came out of the room they'd set up for him. He'd put on his pajamas and was still wearing the hat.

"Let's get you to bed," Marshall said and took Oliver's hand once more. They went back down the hall with Dustin following behind them.

"Where's Pal?" Oliver asked. Just then their dog bounded into the room. He jumped onto the bed as soon as Oliver got in and curled up near his feet.

"He'll probably stay with you," Dustin said as Oliver tried to keep his hat on in bed.

Marshall plucked it off him and placed the hat on one of the bedposts. "That's the cowboy way."

Dustin gave Oliver a hug, and then Marshall did the same as Oliver settled under the covers.

"Good night," Marshall said, watching Oliver roll over, holding a stuffed rabbit close to him. Marshall slowly backed out of the room after Dustin and left the door cracked so Pal could get out. Then he and Dustin quietly returned to the kitchen.

Dustin poured two mugs of coffee and brought them to the table. "Marshall, I think you and I need to talk."

Damn, Marshall knew that tone and what it meant. He also hated those words, because in more than twenty years, the few times Dustin had said something like that… well, things hadn't been good. "I think I know, and…." He took the mug and lifted his gaze to meet Dustin's. Shit, he so did not want to be having one of those awful "this is what's going on in our lives" conversations. He also wasn't so sure what the hell was truly happening. But dammit, he loved Dustin, and he was his partner. Things hadn't been great, but Marshall was no quitter.

Dustin pulled out his chair. Before he sat down, Marshall strode around the table. Dustin stiffened as though he were expecting something bad. Marshall didn't let him react further, just grabbed the collar of his shirt, yanked him forward, and crashed their lips together.

Fuck, that felt good. More than good, it felt *right*, and it was something he had been missing for far too fucking long. He held Dustin there through the second or so that he didn't react, and then Dustin's arms went around his shoulders and Dustin kissed him back, suddenly a live wire. Wow, that was the Dustin he remembered, all energy and *let's fucking go now*.

Dustin tasted the way he remembered, like fire and energy mixed with a touch of chilies from dinner. How had Marshall managed to stay away from him for so damned long?

Marshall backed away. Dustin's eyes were as wide as saucers. Then Marshall tugged him forward once more, taking possession of his mouth while Dustin held on to him for dear life, quivering in Marshall's arms. Marshall lifted Dustin off his feet, and those long legs wrapped around him.

A loud knock sounded from the back door. A few seconds later it came again. Dustin unwound himself and stood on the floor once more. He looked as dazed as Marshall felt. It took a few seconds for the Dustin-induced haze that had formed around him to dissipate.

Then a knock came once more, and Marshall groaned before turning away to see how quickly he could get the hell rid of whoever it was.

Marshall pulled the door open with more force than was necessary, growling as he stared at Patrick.

"Sorry to both of you, but we got a problem."

"What's happened?" Marshall asked, his head clearing.

"A tree fell across some of the north fencing. The herd hasn't found it yet, but we gotta get that tree cut up and hauled away. Then the fence needs to be fixed. If we wait till morning…." He trailed off as Marshall took a deep breath.

"They'll be everywhere." He turned back to Dustin.

"Go on. I'll make a fresh pot of coffee and some food for when you're done. I'd help, but Oliver is here." Dustin turned away just before Marshall headed out the door.

MARSHALL AND the guys cut the tree up for firewood and hauled it to back to the ranch before stacking it on the pile. They wasted nothing at the ranch, and the tree that took out part of their fence would help keep the house warm come the colder months.

"Thanks, guys. This saved us a lot of work tomorrow," Marshall said as they unloaded the last of the wood.

More than once during the evening, he found himself thinking about Dustin and that kiss. Fortunately he'd let one of the guys handle the chainsaw, or he'd probably have ended up cutting something off since his thoughts were elsewhere.

"Sorry to have bothered you. We know you're looking after the neighbor's kid tonight," Patrick said. "How is his brother doing?"

"They had to take him in right away. We hadn't heard by the time I left, but it's not good." Marshall explained as best he could. "I suppose we need to do our best to help them out so they can give him the care he needs." He paused. "I can't imagine what they must be going through."

"Neither can we. Let us know if there's anything we can do to help." Patrick got into his truck and rolled down the window. "It's a good thing what you and Dustin are doing to help." He raised the window and took off down the drive.

Yeah, Marshall had been a real grump about it, but the kid was cute, and he sure seemed to get under Marshall's skin with just one of those smiles. Oliver looked so much like him in that hat. When his real dad had bought it for him, Marshall had wanted to sleep in it too. To him, the hat symbolized being a cowboy, and that was all he ever wanted to be.

Then he'd grown up, because cowboys rode horses, or did rodeo, managed cattle, and most importantly, according to his stepfather, fucked girls. Marshall hadn't fit into that image, and it had created a crisis of identity that he ended up resolving by leaving home. At the time it had been traumatic, but now he realized it had been the right thing to do, because it put him on a path that intersected with Dustin's.

The rest of the guys headed to the bunkhouse, and Marshall strode to the house, which was mostly dark and quiet.

He might have been hoping that Dustin had waited up for him, but that clearly wasn't the case. Still, he quietly went down the hall. Dustin's door stood open partway, like it always did, and Marshall smiled as he pushed it open farther. Dustin lay under the light covers on his side, chest rising and falling rhythmically. He was clearly asleep. Marshall thought about getting undressed and slipping into bed with him, but he paused, wondering if he would be welcome. That notion that he might not be was frightening, and Marshall backed out again. He and Dustin definitely needed to talk.

Chapter 7

DUSTIN WOKE alone, and he wondered why. Oh yeah, he must have fallen asleep. He had purposely left his door open because he intended to stay awake to wait for Marshall, but he still woke alone. He realized that when Marshall had come back in, he'd gone to his own room. Well, that told him quite a bit. It had taken hours before he'd stopped feeling that kiss, and even though the needs of the ranch interrupted like they always did, he had hoped that Marshall would remember it as well. But it seemed that Dustin was mistaken.

He pushed back the covers and got out of bed. The house was quiet and dark. Marshall wasn't up yet, and neither was Oliver. Dustin dressed, left the house, and went out to the barn, heading right upstairs to the hayloft, where he found a mess. Obviously the guys had been busy, but no one had taken the time to keep the loft orderly. Dustin pulled on his gloves and got to work, tossing and shifting bales until the loft made sense and was much less jumbled. He was covered in sweat because heat had started to

build in the loft before he descended to the relative-
ly cool main floor of the barn below. He pulled off
his gloves and took off his hat, then wiped his brow
as Jackson and a few of the other guys arrived. He
waved and headed inside the house for a shower.

"Where have you been?" Marshall asked when
Dustin reached the bedroom portion of the house.
He'd obviously just stepped out of the shower himself and wore only a towel. Time had been good to
Marshall. He was still muscular and trim, strong, if
a little broader around the hips. Dustin glared for a
second. "Sorry. I got up and you weren't here, and I
don't know what to do when Oliver gets up, and…."
He actually seemed nervous.

Dustin felt some of the tension he'd been trying
to work out finally slip away. "I was just out in the
barn. I wanted to check on the horses and ended up
clearing up the mess in the loft. The guys need to
keep things straight up there rather than letting the
bales fall anywhere they like."

Marshall nodded. "Thanks." He leaned forward
and kissed him.

"What was that for?" Dustin asked.

Marshall smiled quickly. "Just because, I guess."
He left the hall, probably to get dressed, and Dustin
grabbed some clothes and used the shower. When he
finished, Oliver was just coming out of the bedroom,
wearing green dinosaur pajamas, Pal at his heels.

"Are Mommy and Daddy here yet?" Oliver
asked, rubbing his eyes.

"Not yet. Why don't you brush your teeth and clean up? Then you can get dressed. What do you like for breakfast? I have eggs and bacon, pancakes…."

"Waffles?" Oliver asked.

Dustin hadn't made them in a while. "I can do that. Marshall likes waffles too, so maybe it's what cowboys really like." Oliver rubbed his eyes again. "Go get dressed and then you can help me in the kitchen… and don't forget your hat. It's a cowboy breakfast."

Oliver went back in the bedroom with a spring in his step, and Dustin hurried to the kitchen to get the ingredients out and the waffle iron ready to go. By the time he was done, Oliver was running into the kitchen with Pal behind him. "Sit down," Dustin told his dog, and then he brought over a stool for Oliver. "Do you want to mix the batter?"

"Is that what cowboys do?" Oliver asked.

Dustin nodded. "Cowboys are always ready and willing to help. Sometimes it's the neighbors, and sometimes…." Marshall came in, and Dustin lost his train of thought for a second. "Sometimes cowboys help in the kitchen."

They shared a smile, and Dustin wondered again what had happened last night. Then he shook his head to clear it… because he was acting like some lovesick teenager or something. He and Marshall definitely needed to talk and maybe clear the air. But they had a young visitor in the house.

"I'm going to—" Marshall began.

"Cowboys help in the kitchen," Oliver interrupted.

Dustin grinned and put the ingredients into the bowl. He got Oliver slowly mixing everything together.

"Is that so?" Marshall asked. "And then what do cowboys do?"

"They could set the table and get out all the good stuff to go on waffles," Dustin said, sharing a wink with Oliver. "That's really good. It's all mixed and ready to go." He sort of liked teasing Marshall a little. It reminded him of how things were when they first met.

Marshall set the table, and Dustin got a batch of waffles in the iron and Oliver at the table, ready for the first ones out. Marshall sat down once he was done, and Dustin brought the first hot waffles to the table. He gave Oliver one section and Marshall three, as the second ones cooked.

"Are you going to have some?" Oliver asked, taking a bite. "Yummy." Marshall helped him with butter and cinnamon sugar. Apparently that was how cowboys ate their waffles.

The second waffle went mostly to Marshall, and Dustin got some of the third. By the fourth one, they were getting full. Dustin was cooking off the rest of the batter as the back door opened.

"You have visitors," Willy said from outside before Anne came in, followed by Richard carrying Noah.

"Daddy, Mommy!" Oliver cried, and Pal barked.

"How is he?" Dustin asked right away.

"Better. They gave him fluids, and he felt much better right away." Anne seemed to collapse into one of the chairs. "It was a false alarm and…." She seemed seconds from crying.

"Noah, are you hungry?" Oliver asked. "The cowboy waffles are really good."

Noah nodded, and thankfully Marshall got more plates as Dustin served them up. "Sit on down. I got plenty."

"We don't want to impose," Anne said.

"You aren't." Dustin brought her and Richard each a plate with a hot waffle and placed the others in the oven to heat back up. "Give me a few minutes."

"Anyone want coffee?" Marshall offered as he started filling mugs. Dustin thanked him softly and got everyone sat down with plates and food. Marshall sat next to Anne, speaking to her quietly. Dustin wondered what was up, but Anne just nodded, and then the kids pulled Dustin's attention.

"I got to see the horses," Oliver told Noah. "They were really big and really nice. I even got to feed one."

"Can I feed one too?" Noah asked. He had on a light hat, and Dustin knew the little boy had lost his hair.

"After you eat, we can take you to the barn," Dustin offered.

Marshall nodded and put the pot back on the coffee maker. "If you'll excuse me, I have a few things I need to do." He left the kitchen, and Dustin wasn't sure if he should be angry with him. Was whatever he needed to do so important that he couldn't take a few minutes? Dustin was getting a little tired of playing second fiddle to the ranch and everything else.

Maybe if Marshall didn't care enough about him to take some time, then Dustin needed to figure out how he was going to go on with the rest of his life.

"These are really good. Thank you," Richard said.

"Where did you get the hat?" Noah asked.

"Mr. Marshall gave it to me. He said a cowboy needs a hat." Little Oliver, bless his heart, took off the hat and gently placed it on Noah's head. "Now you can be a cowboy too." He drank some of the juice Dustin had poured for him, while Dustin made sure everyone had enough to eat.

"Can we see the horses now?" Noah asked.

"Aren't you tired, sweetheart?" Anne asked.

"No, Mommy. I'm awake," Noah answered with a smile and took the last bite of his waffle. "I was hungry." The little guy turned to Dustin. "Fank you for the waffles. They were good."

Dustin carried plates to the sink.

"Well, then, maybe we can go see the horses," Richard agreed. "But you need to finish your juice and drink some water, like the doctor said." Noah did that, and then both boys were out of their chairs. Dustin wiped his hands.

"Then come with me," he said, taking each boy's hand and leading them to the back door.

Out in the yard, he found Marshall standing between their horses, each saddled and ready to go. "I'm sorry. But I thought that maybe the boys would like to take a ride with us."

"Really?" Oliver asked, both boys bouncing with excitement. He turned to Richard, who'd followed them out. "Can we, Daddy?"

Anne nodded as Richard looked to her. "Sure," Richard answered, his voice choked.

"Okay." Dustin knelt to both boys. "What's going to happen is that Mr. Marshall and I are going to get on the horses, and then your daddy is going to lift each of you up. Noah, you'll ride with me, and Oliver will ride with Mr. Marshall. Okay?"

"Yes!"

"Yes!" They jumped up and down like they'd just won a bag full of candy.

Dustin mounted his horse and Marshall did as well, and then Richard lifted Noah up and placed him in front of Dustin. The process followed with Oliver, and then Marshall urged his horse forward and Dustin fell right in behind. "We're just going to walk like this." He held the reins in one hand and Noah with the other. "Is this fun?"

Noah nodded, his hat nearly tumbling off him. "I always wanted to ride a horsey."

"Well, when you're older, maybe Mr. Marshall or I could teach you and Oliver how to ride. If you want to be a cowboy, that is."

Noah nodded again and leaned back against him. Dustin wondered if the excitement was too much for him, but Noah practically vibrated with energy. "Where are we going?"

"I think to the pond." Judging by the path that Marshall was taking. "It's a pretty ride." And not too far.

His horse settled into a rhythm, and Dustin did as well, holding Noah. He lifted his gaze slightly, and it filled with Marshall's backside. Damn, he looked amazing in the saddle. Always had. But now, somehow he managed to look even better than twenty years ago. Back then he'd been cocky, but now it was confidence and experience. The way his body moved was liquid poetry.

"I'd like to have a horse someday," Noah told him, and Dustin hummed.

"I had my first pony when I was a few years older than you. My mom got him for me for my birthday. His name was Gooseberry, and I loved that pony." He leaned forward to check on Noah, who seemed as happy as anything. "You know, the first night I got him, I begged my mom to let me sleep in the barn. She wouldn't let me, but I snuck out first thing in the morning." They reached the edge of the pond and pulled up next to Marshall and Oliver.

"You all having fun?" Dustin asked.

"Yes." Oliver practically bounced in the saddle. Dustin was concerned that Noah might be flagging and figured they didn't need to linger too long. Still, he caught Marshall's gaze.

"It's been a while since we rode together," he told Marshall softly.

"Too long. We need to remedy that." He smiled, and Dustin returned it. "Let's go back now." He turned, and they started the walk back to the ranch. The horses knew the way, and Dustin relaxed slightly, watching Marshall the entire time. For years they had lived together and worked to make a living, but they didn't really have a life. Not the way they had when they were young. Now Dustin felt a touch of that same energy. Marshall was still as handsome and sexy as he'd always been, and Dustin wondered if he was the problem. Maybe he'd done something to drive Marshall away, or maybe Marshall just wasn't interested in him. One thing was for certain: things could not go on between them the way they had. Something needed to change, and Dustin hoped that change didn't mean the end of things.

"You doing okay?" Dustin asked Noah, who nodded.

They rode the rest of the way back. Richard and Anne were waiting in the yard, and as they came to a stop, Richard lifted Noah out of the saddle.

"I got to ride a horse, Daddy." He held on to his dad, grinning from ear to ear.

"What do you say?" Anne asked with a relieved smile.

"Fank you," Noah added, and Oliver echoed it as he went right to his mom.

"Thank you both," Richard said and shook hands with Marshall and then Dustin. "Both boys have been asking about the horses for weeks, and I know they loved it." He held Noah tightly. "We should get home so we can get you a juice box and maybe you can lie down."

"Come on," Marshall told Oliver. "Let's go get your things and you can go home." He held out his hand. Oliver took it, and the two of them going inside.

"I never thought he would warm up to kids, but I think your son has changed all that," Dustin said with a smile.

"Oliver wants to be a cowboy when he grows up," Richard said.

"Does he want the hat back?" Anne asked.

"No. You take it. Marshall gave it to Oliver," Dustin said as they came back out.

"Bye, Mr. Marshall," Oliver said and then crooked his finger to motion him closer. Dustin didn't hear what Oliver asked, but Marshall nodded and then Oliver gave him a hug. It had to be one of the most precious things he had ever seen. Oliver then came over and hugged Dustin before the four of them headed for their car. Both boys waved as their parents carried them and got them inside.

"I have things I need to do," Marshall said and turned away.

"Stop," Dustin snapped. "You need to come inside. There are things we need to talk about, and I'm tired of taking a back seat to whatever it is you need to do all the time. I know there's work, but it will wait a damned hour."

"But—" Marshall began.

"Either you put the horses in the barn and come inside now, or when you get back, I won't be here."

Dustin turned and strode inside. Okay, so his anger had probably gotten the better of him, but he was damned tired of feeling like he wasn't worth a crap and that everything around here was more important than him.

"What's gotten into you?" Marshall asked when they were inside.

Dustin turned, holding the back of one of the chairs. "Sit down," he said, and Marshall pulled out the chair across from him and sat. "Lately I've been unhappy, and I've had thoughts about leaving." He might as well just say what was on his mind. "Do you know how fucking frightening that is?" He waited for Marshall to say anything, but it seemed that Dustin had stunned him. Still, he leaned forward. "We've been together for over twenty years. You and I built this ranch together, and we turned it into this bastion of safety for us and the people who work here. We fought cross-burners together, and lately I've been thinking of walking away." He paused.

"Dustin…," Marshall managed to say.

"Don't you get it? We sleep in separate beds, and you kissed me yesterday. Do you remember the last time you did that? Because I sure as hell don't. So what do you want? Because things can't go on like this. I won't continue to be second fiddle to everything that goes on around here, and I'm not going to sit in here and act like the damned cook and dishwasher. I know a lot of that is my fault. You took on the ranch and threw yourself into it, and I seem to have taken on whatever was left."

"I have to work in order to keep the ranch going and to keep this house over our heads. That's my job, and if I didn't do it, then I wouldn't be providing for the guys here and for you." Now Marshall was steamed, but Dustin could deal with that. Any sort of emotion was better than this dancing around each other.

"It's my ranch too, you know. Managing the business isn't all your responsibility. I'm supposed to be your partner, not the cook. We need to talk about things and work as a team. Do you realize that other than helping our neighbors, you and I haven't done anything together in years?" He was trying to make a point, but maybe he'd gotten on his soapbox a little.

"I work hard around here, and I do that so I can provide for you. I want to make sure that you have a good home and that you don't have to worry about all the shit that I did when I was a kid. I...." Marshall paused and then stood up, nearly tipping the chair over. He stomped around the table and grabbed Dustin by the shirt like he had the day before, holding him in place as he kissed Dustin's breath away.

Dustin released the back of the chair that he had been holding for support, and Marshall pressed him back. Their lips never parted as Marshall propelled him into the other room. Then Dustin took control, using his weight to throw Marshall off a little before pressing him down onto the sofa cushions. He straddled Marshall, gazing into his eyes for a second before crashing their lips together once more. Damn, he tasted better than Dustin remembered, and his entire body throbbed with energy. "It's been way too damned long," Dustin said, his throat scratchy.

Marshall nodded, and Dustin took his lips once again. Hell, this was good. Dustin slipped a hand under Marshall's shirt, sliding along the ridges of muscle built through years of work on their ranch and their land. Those muscles were his, and Dustin intended to get a good close-up look at them. He slid his hand upward, fingers brushing over a taut nipple, then pulled back from Marshall's lips. He rolled the bud between his fingers, pinching slightly. Marshall hissed, but Dustin knew that sound and remembered the way it made Marshall's eyes roll back. "You always loved that."

"Fuck," Marshall drawled out long and slow.

"That's exactly what I had in mind," Dustin whispered back, accentuating his point with another light pinch. Marshall quivered under his touch, and Dustin adored that. He knew damned well what turned Marshall on. What he'd forgotten was how stunningly hot Marshall was like this and what a thrill it was to reduce him to openmouthed, wide-eyed silence.

The back door opened just as Dustin leaned forward and kissed Marshall once more.

"Marshall?"

Dustin straightened up, looking over the back of the sofa just as Patrick stepped into view.

"There's something you—" He stopped when he saw Dustin.

"Is anyone dying?" Dustin snapped. He was so damned tired of the ranch interrupting them. It was starting to feel like a conspiracy.

"No," Patrick answered.

"Can you handle it without Marshall?" he asked, his body shaking.

"Yes." Patrick took a step back.

"Then do it. Now get… the hell… out!" He turned back to Marshall and took possession of his lips before Marshall could say anything. The back door slammed closed, the sound barely registering in his passion-addled brain.

Dustin tugged at the buttons of Marshall's shirt, parting the fabric. He ran his hands over Marshall's chest and then down his belly, just taking in the once-familiar planes of him. Marshall was all hard angles of cowboy muscle. There was nothing soft on him. This body—hell, the man himself—was a product of the land, their land, and a life of hard work. One Dustin wanted to be the one to share going forward.

"Do you want to do this here?" Marshall growled. "Because I'll gladly fuck you right here, make you scream so loud you can't talk for a week." He sat up, tugging the shirt off his arms, and then wrapped them around Dustin, holding him tight. "Is that what you want?"

"Maybe we should go to the bedroom," he answered.

"Which one?" Marshall asked.

Dustin leaned close, his eyes boring into Marshall's. "The one that you want to be ours." He was so tired of this separate beds thing.

Marshall pushing him back and somehow managed to get to his feet, bringing Dustin right along with him. Damn, Marshall had always been strong, but in the past few years, he'd grown powerful. Dustin didn't fight him as Marshall half carried him to his own room. He bounced when Marshall pushed him down on the bed. "Is this what you want?"

"No," Dustin answered, grabbing Marshall by the belt. "Get the fuck down here."

Marshall tugged on the hem of Dustin's shirt, pulling it up. Dustin lifted his arms, and Marshall tugged off the shirt. "You were always the sexiest man I ever saw."

Dustin smiled. There were so many things he wanted to say, but Marshall kissed them all away.

Their movements became frantic, neither able to get the other out of their clothes fast enough, and if there were a few bruises from wayward knees or elbows, it didn't seem to matter. All Dustin wanted was Marshall's skin under his hands, pressed to him. "It's been too long."

"Fuck yes," Marshall murmured when Dustin cupped Marshall's firm ass in his hands, winding his legs around his waist, holding on tight.

Marshall reached to the bedside table and fumbled around the in the drawer until he slammed it closed and slick fingers pressed into him. Dustin hissed and arched his back.

"Too much?" Marshall asked.

"Don't you dare stop," Dustin growled, and then Marshall sank into him. It had been a while, and the burn was exquisite. Dustin closed his eyes and held on, breathing deeply as Marshall slowly sank deeper, filling him, thick, hot, and hard. Holding still, they breathed together until Marshall slowly began to move.

"Damn, how did I get along without this?" Marshall breathed.

"Talk less, fuck more," Dustin countered.

"Before, you wanted me to talk," Marshall teased, and Dustin smacked his shoulder.

"That was then. This is now, and dammit, I want you. So make it good and maybe we'll do this again." Damn, the shocked expression in Marshall's eyes was so worth it.

Marshall stopped, seated deep within. "Is that how you think this works?"

"Don't you dare."

"What?" Marshall snapped.

Dustin drew Marshall down into a kiss that only poured gasoline on the fire between them. "No playing games, just fuck me." Tingles were already starting at the base of his spine, and Marshall flexed his hips before slowly rolling them, sending Dustin damned near into orbit. Dustin wound his arms around Marshall's neck, holding him close as he tried to keep from flying apart.

He wasn't as limber as he'd been in his rodeo days, but Marshall seemed to make the best of it. He'd definitely not lost any of his hip action ability, and Dustin clutched the bedding as Marshall drove him higher and higher. There were few things in life more exciting than that rush of riding an animal that didn't want to be ridden, but this was one of them. This exact moment when two people clicked physically and mentally. Dustin didn't have to say a word about what he wanted—his body communicated it, and Marshall seemed to read each of the cues, knowing what he was in the mood for before Dustin could even say it.

"Yeah…," Dustin whispered, sweat breaking out all over him when Marshall backed away, slowing his movements just as Dustin was nearing the edge. "What are you doing?"

Marshall pulled away just enough for Dustin to still feel his breath. "Remember that night in Denver? We went back to the hotel with that hot tub in the room and I held you on the edge for hours. You moaned and begged until I gave in, and then you shot hard enough to hit the headboard." He grinned.

Dustin gasped. "That was twenty years ago, and I'm nowhere near as young as I was then." Still, he held Marshall tightly, because whatever happened, he was here with him, and that was more than enough for now.

"Give yourself more credit. We're smarter than we were then and just as capable," Marshall whispered, rolling his hips again, and Dustin arched his back, head lolling back as Marshall gripped his cock and stroked hard. Everything seemed to be happening at just the right speed and pressure, because within seconds Dustin was on the edge once again, only this time Marshall powered right through, plunging him into the abyss of ecstasy, and Dustin let himself fall for what seemed like forever until his mind came to rest back on the bed with Marshall next to him.

Dustin sure as hell hoped that Marshall had come when he did, because he had no energy left whatsoever. This was amazing, and he inhaled deeply, desperate for oxygen and to be able to see and think once more. "What the hell?"

Marshall chuckled. "I think we are, in fact, getting older."

"Duh." It was all he could say. There had been a time when he and Marshall would have taken a half hour and been ready to go again. Dustin somehow doubted that was in the cards any longer. "But what a way to go."

Marshall chuckled, deep and resonant. "You can say that again." He sighed, and neither of them moved until Marshall rolled over to face him. "I guess...."

"Yeah... well, I guess you answered some questions for me. But you know that a round of mind-blowing sex isn't going to change much."

"Okay. What is it you want? Do you not want to do the cooking and stuff? I have money in the budget for one more position. I could hire us a housekeeper if I can find one. That way she could do the cooking and cleaning, and you'd have time for more work outside. If that's what you want."

"You just hired someone," Dustin said.

"Yeah, Jackson, and if he doesn't keep his eyes at home and stop staring at my hot partner, he isn't going to be long for this world, let alone working here," Marshall growled.

Dustin rolled to his side, propping his hand under his head. "Is that the reason for the raging hotness? You got jealous and decided to mark your territory? Was this a case of you only wanting something because someone else is interested?" He scowled, ready to take Marshall to the proverbial woodshed.

"You know me better than that. Yes, I'm still pissed at Jackson for sniffing around you, but I can't blame him. You're still as cowboy studly as you were when I first set eyes on you." Marshall slid closer.

"Then why does it seem like I'm the least important thing on this ranch?"

Marshall shook his head. "You aren't a thing. Never were. And I'm doing everything I do for you."

He paused and then sighed. "I promised you a long time ago, when we bought this place, that I would do anything I had to in order to make it a success."

"And you have."

"*We* have," Marshall corrected, and Dustin wondered if he had been seeing things all wrong.

"Okay. But…."

Marshall kissed him. "Sometimes you worry way too much." Marshall smiled that grin of his that always disarmed Dustin in a moment. "Do you remember that final ride in Las Vegas? You were at the top of the standings and had been all year. The top of your game, and you were so nervous."

"Yeah, I was—until I walked into that arena with you. Then I knew what was important." In that moment, Marshall had held his hand for all the world to see, and then he realized that win or lose, Marshall would always be there. Dustin swallowed, because he wasn't so sure of that any longer. "But things change, Marshall. No matter how much we may wish otherwise or how much we say we want it." Dustin knew this was the worst pillow talk of all time, but Marshall had to know that one afternoon of passion wasn't going to change everything.

"Is that what you want? To go your own way?" For the first time in years, Dustin saw fear in Marshall's eyes.

"I didn't say that. But do you want things to go on the way they have the last few years for the rest of our lives? Because that's what we're settling into. The ruts of our routine just get deeper and harder to get anything to change."

"We've been busy building a life," Marshall said. "What do you expect?"

"I don't know. But this isn't a life. We haven't been living. You and I have been working and not really living." Dustin stroked his arm. "I'm not saying that I want to walk away, but we need to figure out what we want. Is what we have—our relationship—worth the effort or not? Because if it is, then both of us are going to need to change. I don't want a life without love and passion. I want to like my life and who I am again. I haven't in a while. And you deserve to be happy and to want to come home at the end of the day."

"What is it you want from me?" Marshall asked.

Dustin hesitated. "I don't know, and I can't give you a list. I want what you're willing to give, and I want to know what's truly important to you." He could only hope that in the end, it was him.

But at least they were talking. That was the first step.

Chapter 8

To say that Marshall was stunned was an understatement. Dustin had wanted to talk, and passion got the better of him. So the talking came afterward, and he didn't know what to make of it. Yes, Dustin had frightened him. But what he didn't understand was that he thought Dustin liked his life and that the ranch and Marshall were what he wanted. Dustin might have had some points in his talk, but it had been Dustin who had backed away from Marshall.

Dustin snored, and Marshall hadn't been able to sleep, so he'd gone to another room to sleep because he needed to get up early to work. Dustin certainly could have come to his room any time he wanted. Marshall purposely kept the door open, and yet Dustin never had. Marshall felt like he had been left behind. For the first time in months, he'd managed to get Dustin's passionate attention, and it had been hot. But then Dustin said it didn't change anything.

"What the fuck was with that?" he muttered as he stomped across the yard toward the equipment shed. The guys were all out on jobs, and the new hand was hard at work. Jackson barely looked up from his task when Marshall came into the barn. Clearly someone had given him a talking-to, which was good, because Marshall didn't need to go firing someone today. In the mood he was in, anyone who crossed him was likely to find their ass out on the street. Being with Dustin changed everything. Why didn't he see that?

Marshall worked his hands to the bone for him. It was the best way he knew to show someone how much they meant. Didn't Dustin know that he'd stand in front of a speeding truck for him? Marshall climbed on the four-wheeler, backed it out of the shed, and took off. The day had been a scorcher—the heat hadn't abated in the least and wasn't likely to for hours yet. The land passed under the wheels, bumping him as he went along, and that was fine. Marshall needed something to jar his mind out of the racing thoughts of Dustin that never seemed to end.

"What are you doing here?" Patrick asked as Marshall pulled up close. "We're just about done. The herd has been well watered, and it looks like the rain was good upstream, because the creek is really flowing." That was always good to hear when the heat built in. "We checked all the pipes and water flow, and it's excellent. Cleaned out some gunk and made sure everything is in top condition."

Marshall nodded. "Good." He'd only been half paying attention, and Patrick had picked up on it.

"What's going on, boss?" Patrick asked. "You should be in a good mood. Dustin was sure growly." He smiled wickedly, and it took all Marshall's willpower not to slug him. Not that he was mad at

Patrick, but he was so wound-up and frustrated, the urge to hit something or someone was almost overwhelming.

"So help me…."

Patrick put his hands up. "Geez. Guys who get laid are usually mellow, so either things fell through or the talking afterward didn't go so well." He stood still, and Marshall groaned.

"I don't know what to do. He says I put the ranch first, but I do this for him and all the guys here. We're a family, and we look after each other."

Patrick's eyes widened. "If we're a family, it's because of Dustin." He was clearly waiting for that to sink in. "You're a good boss, and you see to it that the work gets done and that the guys aren't over-worked. You pay people well for a hard day's work, and we all respect you. But that isn't what makes a family. Dustin always sees that the guys are fed, and on the holidays he makes packages for everyone to take home."

"Huh?" Marshall had never known that.

"Yeah. For the guys that are married, he makes larger boxes so their families have special treats. He makes sure that our families are looked after and watches out for all of us. Do you remember when Phillip got hurt a few years ago? Dustin checked in on his family every day. And when they had to move back with his family, Dustin was there to help them pack up and made sure that they made it okay. It's Dustin who makes this ranch feel like a family." Patrick put his hands on his hips. "And you thought you did that?" He shook his head, chuckling.

Marshall growled.

"See, that's just it. You act like the boss, and the ranch needs that to survive. But it also needs everyone to pull together and care about each other. That's what Dustin does. You feel it, but never realized where it came from. It's the two of you together that make this ranch so special. I'm really surprised you haven't figured that out." Patrick called to the other guys and told them to head back.

"Good work. Thank you," Marshall called as well, and they headed off. "Jesus, what do I do?"

"About what? There's nothing wrong on the ranch. You're an amazing ranch manager, and you treat the men fairly. There's nothing to change there. You and I work well together, and I oversee a lot of the work as foreman. It's your job to plan for the future, and you do that better than just about any rancher I've ever met. You have a vision for this place and know how to move it forward five, even ten years. But sometimes you don't see what's right in front of you." Patrick shrugged. "Nobody's perfect. I know I'm not."

"But what the hell?" Marshall asked. "It's like everyone has turned on me. I thought I was doing the right thing, and…."

Patrick shrugged. "My dad always told me that life was about balance. If you spent too much time working, then the other parts of your life suffered. If you spent too much time in bed doing the horizontal hula, then the work suffered." He could just hear Caleb saying that. He had been the foreman when Marshall and Dustin had bought the ranch. Years ago, he and Mildred had moved to Arizona to retire, and Patrick had moved into the job. There were times when Marshall still missed Caleb. He was one of those people he felt he could talk to, and there weren't many people like that in his life. Marshall always thought he could talk to Dustin about just about anything, but it seemed that the two of them had stopped talking—at least about what was important, anyway, if Dustin could take him by surprise like that. "What you need to do is find some sort of balance."

"That's easy for you to say. What sort of balance do you have in your life?" Marshall quirked his eyebrows.

"It's simple. I work here during the day, and on my days off, I go into town and have a good time. There are plenty of places in Dallas where a real cowboy can have a really good time. I let off some steam, come home, and go back to work." He grinned wryly. "No muss nor fuss."

"Is that the kind of life you really want to have? Work here, play there? What about a wife and kids?"

"Maybe eventually. I haven't met anyone I want to marry. As for kids, I love them—especially someone else's, so when they act up, I give them back to Mom and Dad and go on my merry way. See? Balance."

Marshall rolled his eyes. "You're an ass."

"Hey. I know the way I live isn't for you. But I like it, and I have balance. If I meet a woman that I really like and want to date, then I will, and the balance in my life will be shot to hell until I figure it out. You just figure out your balance. You work all the time, and maybe that's taking away from you and Dustin. He's important to you, right?" Marshall nodded. "Then you need to make time for him. Spending money on someone is one thing; working is another. But the time you spend with someone, doing things together… my dad always said that was why he and Mom stayed together. They did things they liked, and then he got the hell out of the house so she didn't cut his balls off."

Marshall groaned loudly. "You're a big help."

Patrick shrugged. "If Dustin is important, then treat him like he is. It's not hard. You've always treated the ranch and the work like they were important, and the ranch is thriving. Maybe you stopped acting like Dustin is important, and that's why things probably feel a little rocky."

"How do you know so much about relationships if you're single?" Marshall asked.

"It's simple. Haven't you noticed that it's always easier to see other people's problems than your own?" He grinned. "Now, I think I better get back to the ranch before my boss catches me jawing out here and has a fit."

"Asshole," Marshall called without any heat. "Go on and get back before the guys run amok. I'll be right behind you to make sure Jackson doesn't try to run off with my partner."

Patrick laughed. "I told him to keep his eyes and mouth to himself if he wanted to live through the week. It seems he was the belle of the rodeo ball and is used to getting all the attention he wanted. I told him if he wants that type of attention, there are places in Dallas he could go. He needs to learn that you don't fish where you live. Not if you want to keep eating." He hopped on his four-wheeler and took off with a wave.

Marshall lifted his hat off his head, wiped his brow, and plopped it back on. It seemed Jackson had gotten the message about his partner. Now all Marshall had to do was figure out how to make Dustin happy once again. It couldn't be that hard. Dustin wasn't a complicated man. Just as he climbed on his four-wheeler, he hit on an idea.

"HOW IS Noah doing? Have you heard?" Marshall asked Dustin a couple days later after lunch, once the others had left the table. Dustin sat diagonal from him, and Marshall reached out and took his hand. It seemed kind of childish to hold hands, but when his fingers slid along Dustin's, it felt right, and he was glad he'd done it, especially when Dustin's gaze followed the touch.

"I talked to Anne this morning, and she said that he was doing well. His next treatment is in a few days. They always hit him hard, but that one should be the last in this round. Then she said they'll wait to see if the treatment has been successful or if they have to do something else." Dustin squeezed his fingers. "I can't imagine what they're going through with all this. The ups and downs have to be scary as hell. I rode broncs and you rode bulls, and I'd rather do either of those things at my age than go through what they are." He sipped his coffee.

"Well, our anniversary is coming up in a few weeks. It will be twenty-five years since I walked into that arena and saw you on that bronc for the very first time. We didn't talk, but I remember that first time I saw you. Always will." He squeezed Dustin's fingers. "There's a rodeo in Fort Worth that weekend, and I have a buddy who's willing to help me get tickets. In fact, they're interested in having us make an appearance. Especially you, as a former world champion."

"That would be nice. It's been a while since we did something like that." Dustin's smile shone even in his eyes.

"We can get a hotel and spend an entire day away from the ranch… and I was thinking… we could get two hotel rooms and see if Anne and Richard want to come along and bring the boys. Can you imagine the two of them and all the real cowboys?"

Dustin's smile got brighter if that was possible. "Are you serious?"

"Sure. We can ask them later today. I wanted to run the idea by you before I went ahead and did it. I didn't know what you'd think. Maybe it's too much for Noah."

Dustin shrugged. "I saw them yesterday in town, and Noah was with them. They were having lunch at the diner. They were just leaving, with Noah asleep on his dad's shoulder, when I ran into them. They wanted to try to give Noah some fun before he had that next treatment." He paused. "I think it's a great idea." Dustin squeezed Marshall's hand in return before pulling it away.

"Yeah… okay, I have some work to do." He knew he was escaping into ranch work, but he didn't know what else to do. He felt a little vulnerable at the moment, and that was the easiest way for him to handle it. Dustin cocked his eyebrows just so. Why was it that he could challenge him without saying a goddamned word? "What do you want from me?" Marshall asked, his belly doing little flips that he hated.

Dustin leaned over the table. "You don't need to be afraid of me. Sometimes I wonder how far we've grown apart when you can't talk to me about things that make you uneasy." Damn, those eyes flared with heat and anger. Dustin was hot that way. "Sometimes I want to just scream at you. But that wouldn't do any good."

"Probably not," Marshall sniped.

"All I want to know is, what are you afraid of? We've known each other for a quarter century, and now you're fucking afraid to talk to me. Give up the macho cowboy crap and just tell me, because this vanishing into the ranch to get away from whatever it is that makes you nervous is getting old and is going to cost you in a big way."

There it was—the threat that Marshall had known was coming eventually. Not that it surprised him, but he didn't know what to do about it.

"Remember those ruts we talked about? Well, there it is. When something makes you unsure, you run away into work and use it to hide from everything." Dustin's gaze flared with fire, and Marshall braced himself for a further tongue-lashing, but instead Dustin put his hand on his cheek. "You don't need to be afraid of me and what I'm going to think. I already know you… the real you."

Marshall shrugged. "It's just easier to do the work than to say the words. Okay?" He didn't mean to snap. "It's part of who I am."

"What? A closemouthed pain in the ass everyone spends all their time trying to read because you don't do anything other than issue orders and then get to work? You have to know that I do that. So do the men… all of them. We spend more time trying to figure out if Marshall is angry or upset or happy or fucking horny, because you don't tell anyone anything. And it's hardest for me. So"—he pointed toward the door—"go issue your instructions to the men and get to work rather than talk to me."

"Is that what you think I do?" Marshall asked, stunned. "I work hard because I want to provide for you. I want to give you the best life I can." He inhaled deeply. His life suddenly felt it was in the middle of quicksand and about to go under and be lost forever. "I work hard… to exhaustion sometimes, and I do that for you. I do it because you're the most important piece of my life." His anger rose, but Marshall tamped it down. "I do it because I love you." There, he had said the words. "I hope you're fucking happy." Marshall huffed like he'd just run a marathon.

Dustin grinned from ear to ear. "Was that so hard to say?"

"Yes… no… maybe…?" He humphed. "But I shouldn't have to say it, because I show it to you every single day." He blinked, staring at Dustin, wondering why he just couldn't understand that.

Everything he did was for Dustin and his family. His family might be just him and Dustin, but that was all he needed, and the thought of it going away frightened him to the core.

Dustin's eyes were wide, and his mouth hung open slightly as though the notion had never occurred to him. "But you used to tell me how you felt all the time," he whispered. "I remember that hotel outside Casper. That tacky tourist place with every western cliché in its decoration? The Bronco Buster Motor Lodge." He smiled. "I will never forget that place because it was where you first told me that you loved me. You know, not everyone is the same, and sometimes people need to hear how you feel." Dustin's expression softened. "But I hear you about the things you do, and I can see you're making an effort." He stroked Marshall's cheek. "And I love you too. Always have."

"Then what happens how?" Marshall asked.

Dustin snorted. "Like I have all the answers. I don't know. We have to figure shit out one day at a time. It's too easy for everything to go back to how it was." He pulled his hand away. "You go on and get done what you need to. I'll go talk to Anne and Richard, and I'll see you later."

"But you just said…," Marshall began, and then faltered. "Sometimes I think I will never understand you."

"It's not hard. You told me how you felt. That's all I wanted. And I know after something like that, you'll want to go out there and throw something around or just work yourself into a frenzy so you can get out the frustration I can already see building in your eyes. And that's okay. I get frustrated too sometimes. I miss working with the animals and with my hands, because I want to feel like a cowboy too." He sighed, having gotten that out. "Go punch some cattle because you love me." He grinned, and Marshall thought that Dustin was beginning to understand.

Marshall stood and went to leave the room before pausing. He then went back to the table, leaned over Dustin, and when he turned toward him, he took Dustin's lips with everything he had. This wasn't a kiss to claim him or one to start something he didn't have time to finish. This was a kiss of promise… to let Dustin know what was coming later. When he pulled back, he met Dustin's heated gaze, flashed a smile, and then strode out of the kitchen, snagging his hat along the way. "You wanna come? We can punch cows together."

Chapter 9

"ARE YOU serious?" Anne asked that evening when Dustin and Marshall brought over a dish of his special mac and cheese. The boys sat at the table, eating and talking nonstop. It seemed they loved the gooey meal, just like the hands, who practically vacuumed the dish clean every time he made it.

"Mommy, come eat," Oliver called.

"I'll be right there," she answered. "You're really serious?" she asked more softly.

"Of course we are. Dustin and I were asked to attend as guests. Well, mostly Dustin, because he was world champion." Dustin couldn't help sharing a glance with Marshall. There had been times when he'd been afraid that Marshall would be jealous of the fact that he had won the title in his event. Marshall had come so damned close. "But we thought that we'd go in one vehicle, and getting an extra hotel room would be no problem."

Dustin peered into the kitchen, where Oliver and Noah sat. Oliver wore his hat and ate like a fiend. Dustin made a mental note to get Noah a hat of his own. "The boys seemed so interested in anything cowboy. And they could see a real rodeo. We still have friends on the circuit, so they could meet them."

"I already made a reservation for the rooms because I wanted to make sure we had them." Marshall flashed his best smile, and Dustin saw Anne's hesitation slipping away. "We also figured since it's in Fort Worth, it will be close enough to Dallas that if anything happens with Noah, we can get him there right away." Damn, Marshall had thought of everything, it seemed. "You don't need to decide right away. Talk it over with Richard and let us know. I can cancel the extra room."

Anne seemed overwhelmed. "Why are you doing this?" she asked. "What do you want from us?" She bit her lower lip, suspicion darkening her eyes.

"Nothing," Dustin explained when it seemed Marshall was at a loss for words. "I know you haven't lived out here for long, and that's the city in you talking. But here, we help one another. And if you decide to stay here long-term, those boys of yours are going to grow up cowboys. It's all around them and what the life is out here. People work the land here. It's how we make our living and what the town is based on."

"And friends make good neighbors," Marshall added.

Some of the tension slipped from Anne's shoulders. "Okay. I'll talk to Richard about it, but I think it's a good idea. The boys will love it." She leaned forward. "But you know that it depends on how Noah is doing."

"Of course," Marshall said. "Just let us know what Richard says when he gets home, and we can finalize the arrangements." He clapped his knees. "Dustin and I should be getting back." He stood just as both boys raced into the room in sock feet.

"Can we ride the horses again?" Oliver asked, with Noah bouncing on his heels. It was so cute the way they looked up at Marshall like he was the center of the world and the keeper of all horses.

"Not right now, boys. You need to finish eating, and then you can play for a little while before getting ready for bed. Mr. Marshall and Mr. Dustin will be around, and maybe after you have your last treatment, we can see if they have some time."

"Of course," Marshall said, squatting down to both of them. "We'll have you over for a horse ride again. And maybe that time we can take you out to see the cattle and maybe the bull." Marshall made a snorting sound that had both boys giggling. "For now, you do as your mama says, because cowboys are always good to their mamas." He got a hug from each of them, and then they ran back into the other room to finish eating.

"Thank you for that," Anne said as she showed them to the door.

Marshall nodded as he got to his full height, knees popping a little. "I remember how things were. When I was a youngster like that, I wanted everything cowboy just like them." It was too bad that Marshall's dreams had come about in such a harsh way. Both Dustin and Marshall had paid a price for their rodeo dreams, and the sound of Marshall's

joints was a stark reminder of that, just like the stiff-
ness Dustin experienced on colder mornings. The
pains and aches weren't going to go away.

"Have you thought about mutton busting?"
Dustin asked.

"What's that?" Anne asked, a little worried.

Dustin and Marshall chuckled. "It's for the kids.
They ride sheep. I'll check to see if they have that in
Fort Worth. Sometimes they'll have junior rodeo. It's
a real hoot. I'll have to see if we have any pictures of
us. I remember mutton busting a few times. Mostly
so my family could get pictures. I remember it being
fun, but I was always raring to get on my pony and
then my horse. My mother hated that I wanted to ride
bulls." A cloud passed over Marshall's features, but
it didn't stay long.

"I guess I have a lot to learn about this country
life."

Dustin shook his head. "Nope. Just remember
that your nearest neighbor isn't right next door, but
can be miles away sometimes. And help can take
even longer. So don't hesitate to call if you need
anything."

Marshall tipped his hat like the well-mannered
cowboy he was, and Dustin did the same. Then they
left the house and went to the truck.

"I bet your mama was proud of you even if she
was scared," Dustin said. "What isn't there to be
proud of?" He climbed into the cab and pulled the
door closed. Dustin meant what he said. Whether
they said it or not, how could his folks not have been
proud of him? Still….

Marshall humphed. "I ceased to exist after… well… you know what happened."

"Yeah, I know. They were idiots. But that doesn't mean that they didn't go around bragging to everyone about what you did. They just didn't tell you about it… I'm betting." Dustin didn't know for sure, but sometimes he heard rumors. Mostly what he wanted to do was shake Marshall's family until their teeth rattled. Not that it mattered—they were dead, and shaking their old, moldy corpses would be kind of gross. *Water under the bridge*, he told himself a few times until Marshall turned into the yard.

Marshall pulled the truck to a stop and got right out. Dustin expected him to stomp off, but he leaned against the side of the truck, holding his head. Dustin came right around to him. "What's wrong?"

"Nothing," he answered too quickly.

"You know that's bullshit," Dustin said, calling him out.

Marshall straightened up, his face a mask of fury. "Why couldn't we have had parents like them? Why did I have to end up with a mother who couldn't see past the end of her nose and a stepfather who was a complete pile of shit? I didn't ask for him to be part of our lives. Why did my mother not see what he was?"

Dustin knew Marshall had asked himself those same questions many times over the years, but this was one of the few times he'd actually said anything out loud.

"We don't get to pick our parents or our blood family. But we do get to choose the people we spend our time and our lives with. Remember that. It's not what we're born into that counts, but what we make."

MARSHALL WORKED until almost sundown, and when he came in, he was still growly. Dustin fed him the pork chops and mashed potatoes he'd made for dinner and then got everything in the dishwasher and set it running before staring out the kitchen window into the darkness. There wasn't much moon, so out here, there was very little light, and the sky seemed to close around the house like a blanket on a warm night. Dustin heaved in a deep breath and released it slowly, thinking about nothing and everything.

A light knock on the back door barely intruded on his deliberations, and soft voices reached his ears, but he couldn't hear what Marshall and most likely Willy were talking about. After a minute or so, it grew quiet again.

"Dustin," Marshall said.

Dustin turned around and looked into the warm eyes of a slight woman with years of wind and sun coloring her face. "I'm sorry," he said right away, snapping out of his daze. "Can I help you, ma'am?"

"I think I'm here to help you," she said.

Marshall intervened. "This is Willy's aunt, Delta Morris." She held out her hand, and Dustin took it, surprised to find a tight grip in the handshake. "She stopped by to talk about being our housekeeper."

Dustin lifted his gaze to Marshall. He remembered Marshall saying something about hiring one, but he figured it was just a passing idea. Now here was a strange woman in his kitchen. Suddenly he felt very territorial, and his hackles rose. Remembering his manners again, he motioned to the table and offered her a cup of coffee. This was just like Marshall. He was always a problem solver, which meant that instead of talking to Dustin about the issue, he went out and tried to solve it himself rather than just listening. Sometimes Dustin felt like he was at his wits' end because he didn't listen.

"No, thank you. Ranch coffee this late keeps me up all night," Delta answered before taking a seat. "Look, young man," she said. "William said you boys were looking for a housekeeper. I've been doing that in one way or another since I was sixteen years old."

"William?" Dustin asked.

"Yes, William. I raised that boy after his parents were killed in that accident, and he did nothing but give me trouble. He missed his mama and papa something fierce, and it all just burst out all the time. I think it was my cooking that finally won him over... and eventually horses." She smiled slightly, her eyes growing warm as though she was remembering better times.

"May I ask why you're here? I mean...." He shifted his gaze to Marshall for a little help.

Delta sighed and the better times shifted away again, her eyes darkening slightly. "Marvin, my husband, died last year, and what little we had is gone. Marvin, the stupid, gentle, loving, always-trying-to-make-me-happy son-of-a-bitch never passed a greasy meal he didn't want seconds of, and it caught up with him. The money is gone, and I need to work to make my way. I had to sell the house because I couldn't pay the mortgage and eat."

"I see. All right. Let's start with the cooking. What kinds of things do you make? There are favorites around here, and—"

Delta grinned. "I know. William told me about them. As for cooking, I can make just about anything. I also bake, and I don't believe in bland food. Maybe tomorrow I could come over and make you all lunch. As for housekeeping, I don't believe in dust or dirt, so don't go tracking mud on my clean floors." She seemed determined. "I change the beds once a week, and I don't go snooping into other people's business."

Dustin glanced at Marshall. "You do realize that Marshall and I are…." He couldn't find the words—it had been quite a while since he'd had to explain their relationship to anyone.

"Do you think you're the first gay couple I've known?" She rolled her eyes, and Dustin liked her for that. "I'm a good cook. Just ask William. He certainly didn't starve or want for anything in that department."

"Okay. We'll have you come by tomorrow and cook for us. Dustin has been doing the cooking and things like that for a while, but with the ranch continuing to grow, his expertise is needed out in the field." Marshall turned to Dustin. "I've been thinking that maybe we should branch out a little. You and I have the experience and background, so I was thinking you could start a rough stock program. We have the space and the experience. Just because we haven't used it up until now...." He cocked those eyebrows, and suddenly Marshall became all for him. Delta might not have been there at all.

The sound of a throat clearing pulled him out of his daydreams. "It sounds to me like you boys have some talking to do."

Dustin turned to her. "No argument there, but yes, please come back tomorrow. You can make lunch for us and the men and we'll go from there. Do you need a place to live?"

She lowered her gaze. "I've been staying with William's brother and his two kids." Suddenly she seemed like she was on her last nerve.

"We'll take that as a yes," Marshall interjected. "Don't worry, we'll be able to work out a place for you here, and we promise not to put you in the bunk-house." He grinned, and Delta thanked them both and got to her feet.

"Thank you." She left by the back door, and soon headlights slid past the front of the house.

"What do you think?"

"If she can really cook, then we should hire her. And as for the rough stock, can we afford that kind of initial investment?"

Marshall nodded. "You know the Winstons on the other side of town?"

"Who doesn't? They've been in the rough stock business for years. They supply a lot of the bulls and broncos for many of the top rodeos all across the country. Why?" Dustin leaned across the table.

"Karl Winston is getting up there in years, and as you might know, they had one daughter, and she's a doctor in Houston. There's no one to leave the business to. He approached me the other day about us taking over his operation," Marshall said.

Dustin narrowed his gaze. Was this Marshall's way of buying him out of the ranch and saying he wanted out? He could see the solution clear as day. They'd buy the Winston place. Dustin would run that ranch and the operation there, Marshall would run the ranch here, and they would never need to see each other except to discuss business and shit. Not only would they be sleeping in separate bedrooms, but they'd be staying on opposite ends of town. "Is that what you want? Separate places like that?"

Marshall leaned forward. "What the hell is going through your mind? Do you want that? To move out?" He pushed back the chair, and it nearly toppled over. "I thought we were doing better, and…." Marshall grew pale.

"No. Hold it. Let's not both jump to conclusions. I think I did that enough of that for both of us." He knew he was guilty of it. Damn, that showed just how much trust they had lost over the years. It was really funny how silently something could slip away, and then bam… you count on it and… it's gone. "Why don't you tell me what you were thinking?"

"Well, we'd need to talk some more. But Karl would like to retire in the next year or so. He was just putting out a feeler. We don't have to do this, but we could buy his stock and bring it here. We'd have to set up some corrals and a ring, which would mean looking for some more land, but that's doable. We'd need to get good men, and I suspect some of Karl's people would be interested in coming over. He's had men who have been with him for a long time, and he's concerned about them. I was not in any way thinking of trying to run two separate ranch operations." He shook his head. "I'm not that crazy." That flash of a smile was back, and Dustin's insides relaxed.

"How would all this work?" Dustin was trying to get his head around it. The whole thing seemed like a lot of risk to take on, and he wasn't sure he was up for it.

"We'd have to look at things, finances and all that. But it's an opportunity to diversify, and it would give you a part of the operation that you would be in charge of that plays to your unique strengths." He took Dustin's hand. "I'm trying to change things. I really am. You and I don't need to make any decision today. It was something he approached me about when I was in town this morning. I think he wants to know that his operation will be in good hands after he's gone." Marshall squeezed his hand. "We'll talk about it some more and review all our finances. If we do this sort of thing, I don't want us to take on a bunch of debt. We've worked for years to pay off what we had."

"You seem really excited about this," Dustin said.

"I am, I guess. Our ranch is doing very well. We're selling our beef at top prices to the top suppliers, and I don't want to do anything to jeopardize that. But you keep saying that we're in a rut, and maybe it's true. We're not over the hill, so maybe we need a new challenge, and this would certainly be one. It would mean some travel with the animals to rodeos and maintaining the stock's numbers. But it's something we can do." His eyes sparkled, and Dustin found himself nodding. "Is it something that you'd like to do?" Marshall asked.

"I know you said that if we do this, it would be mine to manage, and...." The idea did have its appeal. The beef operation was Marshall's domain, and while Dustin wanted to get more involved in the operation of the ranch, Marshall was the one in charge. It would be nice to have something he could run on his own. "Can I think about it?"

Marshall grinned. "Yes. Of course. There's no hurry. Karl isn't putting the ranch on the open market. He approached us specifically, and he agreed to give us some time."

Dustin sighed. "It's going to take a lot of planning and...." His voice trailed off. Part of him was excited, and yet maybe he was the one who was really settled in his ways, because the idea of change scared him. From what Marshall had said, they were in a really good financial position, and he didn't want to jeopardize that. "I guess I'm a little worried about taking on even more." He held Marshall's hand tighter. "Do you remember those first few years here? We looked after our own cattle and worked together to dig the retaining pond. I mucked out stalls in the evenings because we needed all day to get the cattle work done." He had never been so tired in his life, but he and Marshall had been working for themselves to build a life and a future, which they had.

"Yeah, I do. And maybe I'm being stupid, but I want to look into this to see if we can make this work. But if we decide to do this, it can be something that we do together."

And just like that, Dustin began to get it. This wasn't just a business opportunity—it was Marshall reaching out to find something the two of them could work at.

"We'll sit down with the accountant and talk it over once we're sure this is something we want to pursue."

"Okay. We'll look into it." He slipped his hand out of Marshall's and cleaned up the kitchen before turning out the lights. Marshall went to his office to continue his work. Dustin watched a little television, occasionally glancing toward the office, before eventually turning out the lights and going off to bed.

DUSTIN LAY in bed quietly, with Pal in his usual spot on the floor. He was tired, and sleep came easily when he closed his eyes.

"Is something wrong?" Dustin whispered when he realized Marshall was in the room with him. There was no answer, but the covers lifted and cool air slid down his body as Marshall slipped under the covers next to him and shifted closer. "What...?"

"Hey. Everything is okay. I just missed you," he whispered, and Marshall's rough hands slid over his belly and then tugged him nearer.

"Oh." He burrowed under the covers, pressing close to Marshall as the air-conditioning kicked on, blowing more cool air into the room. "I'm glad."

"You are? I wasn't sure I'd be welcome," Marshall whispered.

Dustin lifted his head off the pillow and pressed Marshall onto his back before straddling him, his bare chest pressing to Marshall's. "You were always welcome." Then Dustin closed the distance between them and captured Marshall's lips as a deep, resonant moan filled the room. "You have to know that. This was our bed for years, and I know I snored, but you left it. But it was always ours, and—"

Marshall cut off his words, circling his arms around Dustin and pulling him tighter. "I know things aren't perfect, and they may never be, but I don't want our ruts to dictate the rest of our lives."

Dustin agreed with that wholeheartedly. But as much as he tried to stop it, a huge yawn overcame him, and he rested his head against Marshall's shoulder. "The spirit is willing—more than willing—but the body is weak." It had been a long day, and he was just so tired.

"I'll still be here in the morning." Marshall rolled onto his side, taking Dustin along with him, and they both settled in bed. "You don't need to worry about that."

"Yeah. I know. But maybe you do. It seems Jackson still has the hots for me, and you know, he's a real looker."

"What? Are you going to trade me in for a younger model?" God, there were times when he felt so close to Marshall—like when Marshall actually got his humor.

"I was thinking about it. But then I'd have to break him in and explain all the finer points of what was important. And he's so young, and guys like that are jackrabbits. They have no patience, and they don't know the beauty of taking their time." He placed his hand on Marshall's cheek. "So I think I'll keep my current model and see if I can update him just a little bit. And while I'm at it, I'll try for an update of my own."

"Does that mean that things are good between you and me?" Marshall asked.

"We're getting there. Maybe you and I can work toward great again. Be there for each other, maybe even build back the personal trust we seem to have lost."

Marshall held him tighter, and Dustin took that as a yes from his sometimes silent partner.

Chapter 10

"ARE WE there yet?" Oliver asked from the very back of the huge SUV that Marshall drove. Rather than try to take everyone in one of the ranch vehicles, Marshall had gotten a rental for a few days. The boys were in their car seats in the second and third rows, with one of their parents next to each of them.

"No, buddy. But it isn't going to be too long now," Marshall promised. Not that Fort Worth was all that far. Oliver was excited as all heck, but Noah had fallen asleep almost as soon as they got on the road.

Marshall and Dustin had both worried right up until the last day or so that Noah wouldn't be up to the trip. His last treatment had been particularly hard on him. Marshall had gone over to sit with him a few times and tell him "cowboy" stories. Most of the time Noah had fallen asleep halfway through them. But in the past week or so, his parents reported that he seemed stronger and stayed awake a lot more, and that he even started playing and laughing once again, which they said was a good sign.

"We'll stop at the hotel first so you all can get checked in and Noah can rest if he needs to. Then we thought we'd all take the boys to the Stockyards to see the cattle drive at four, look around the historic district, and then have dinner." Dustin smiled.

"Daddy," Noah said from right behind him, "are there going to be cowboys there?" Apparently he was awake.

"Yes. Real cowboys who drive cattle," Marshall answered. In actuality it was a show put on for tourists, but they used real Texas longhorns and cowboys on horseback, so it was a *good* show. "We'll be at the hotel in twenty minutes or so." The traffic was getting heavy, and Marshall followed the GPS instructions to the Marriott near the arena. He hated city driving, but he'd be damned if he'd let anyone know. Heck, Marshall probably should have let Richard drive this part of the trip, but the directions seemed straightforward, and once he'd silenced the constant chatter of the GPS and just used the screen, he was fine.

"Are we here?" Oliver asked once Marshall pulled in under the entrance portico.

"Yes, we are," Dustin answered, and everyone began the process of getting out of the vehicle and getting the luggage. Once they had everything, Marshall handed the keys to the valet, and they all went inside. Marshall sent Dustin to get them checked in, while the rest stayed with the luggage.

"There are cowboys everywhere," Oliver said, gaping. Apparently a lot of the rodeo personnel were using the hotel, and men in jeans, cowboy hats, and large prize buckles abounded. Oliver bounced in his dad's arms and then held out his hands to Marshall, who took him.

"Thanks," Richard said. He hurried off, probably to find a bathroom.

"Yes, there are," Marshall agreed with Oliver as one of the passing cowboys paused right in front of him.

"You're Marshall Brand," he said, extending his hand. Marshall shifted Oliver slightly and shook hands. "I'm Catch Karlsen. I'm riding the bulls tomorrow. I was studying some of your rides just the other day. When I heard you were going to be here, I hoped I'd meet you." He smiled genuinely. "Is this your son?" He shook Oliver's hand too.

"No. This is Oliver, and that grinning little guy is Noah. Their mother, Anne, and the boys' father will be right back. Dustin and I don't have any children." Marshall made sure to meet Catch's eyes. It was funny, but sometimes telling people about him and Dustin was a little like coming out all those years ago, and he still got that flutter of uncertainty in his belly. Would the person he was talking to take offense? Would they be derogatory? Sometimes he wondered if he'd ever stop feeling that touch of worry. Catch's smile told him he didn't need to be concerned, and the desire in his eyes as he turned to look at Dustin making his way over set Marshall's teeth slightly on edge.

"You're Dustin Meyers," Catch said as Dustin joined them. He went on to introduce himself with the same enthusiasm. Then he turned to Marshall, glanced back to Dustin... and Marshall saw the instant something clicked in his head and he realized the two of them were together. For a second Catch met his gaze, eyes growing heated, and damned if he didn't wink. At least Marshall thought he did. "It's good to meet you folks."

"Catch is riding bulls tomorrow," Marshall explained to Dustin after swallowing hard. Richard returned, and Oliver went right into his daddy's arms.

"I got the room keys," Dustin said.

"It was good meeting you, Catch," Marshall said. "Good luck tomorrow." He tipped his hat, and Catch did the same. Then they made their way to the elevators, and only once the doors slid closed did Marshall release the tension in his belly. Damn, he was grateful to be away from that gaze.

"You okay?" Dustin asked.

Marshall shook off the weird feeling as they rode upward. "I'm fine." He flashed Dustin a smile and rubbed the back of his neck. Maybe it was just surprise that a young guy like Catch would find him attractive. Hell, that look in Catch's eyes had been pure heat and desire. From a guy twenty years younger—a fucking kid. Why in the hell did that thrill him so much? Marshall shifted slightly closer to Dustin and waited for the elevator to reach their floor, knowing he was stupid for making such a big deal out of the whole thing. It was just a brief look and didn't mean anything.

Once the elevator doors opened, they trooped their luggage and the boys down the hall to their rooms, which were across the hall from each other.

Marshall checked his watch. "Do you want to meet in the lobby in an hour? We can go to the Stockyards from there. That should give us enough time to get a place to park, and we can see the cattle drive."

"That's sounds good," Richard said and unlocked the door. Both boys hurried inside, with Richard pulling in the luggage.

"Thank you both for this," Anne said gently. "The boys have been so excited about this, and I know it's helped Noah. He's been determined to see the rodeo and all the cowboys. It's also the only time away we've had since Noah's diagnosis." She seemed so worn out.

"We're glad to do it," Marshall said. "Go on and get a little rest, and we'll meet you in an hour."

Dustin already had their room open and the luggage inside. Marshall went in and found Dustin with his boots and hat off, lying on his side of the king bed.

"I saw the way Catch was looking at you," Dustin said without opening his eyes. Marshall hummed his agreement, pushing down the hint of excitement at the notion. "You liked it, didn't you?" Marshall wasn't sure if Dustin was angry.

"I guess it was flattering." He might as well be honest. Marshall put Dustin's suitcase on the stand and hauled his to the other side of the bed. He set his hat on the chair and opened his bag, then carried his kit to the bathroom. "No more than Jackson's interest had to be flattering to you." Two could play this game.

"Catch sure as hell wanted you to be a hell of a lot more than flattered." Dustin came up behind him in the bathroom, his expression almost thunderous in the mirror. Marshall geared up for a fight until Dustin broke into a grin. "Maybe he was looking for a daddy."

Marshall gaped and would have gotten angry except for Dustin's smile. Damn his teasing.

"Could you just hear him? 'I want you, Daddy. Take me, Daddy. I'm a baaaaaad boy.'" Dustin smacked his butt and turned away, laughing like a loon. Then he returned with his own kit and set it next to Marshall's. "Did that turn you on? Do you want to be that youngster's daddy?" He slipped his arms around Marshall's waist. "I didn't even realize that Jackson had any interest in me."

"You didn't?" Marshall asked.

Dustin shook his head. "Maybe it's just been so long since I felt sexy in that way that I didn't realize what his looks meant. Or maybe it's because I already have a cowboy of my own at home." He leaned against him, resting his head on Marshall's shoulder blades. "But I'd say something was different for you." There were times when Dustin could be completely oblivious. Marshall wished that this was one of those. "He caught your attention." A slight tension slipped into Dustin's tone.

Marshall turned around. "It doesn't matter that I'm flattered by him. It also doesn't matter what Catch thinks or wants. He's a young man who lets his little head guide the rest of him." He smiled slightly. "You remember what that was like."

"I do. That's part of what has me concerned." Dustin swallowed. It was funny—if they had been

yelling at each other, Marshall could understand
the disagreement they were having. But they both
seemed calm, too damned calm, and that was part
of what worried him. Did Dustin not care enough
that another man was interested in him? Did it really matter so little? The fact that Jackson watched
Dustin had made him want to wring the man's neck
on a few occasions.

"You don't sound concerned. Hell, maybe you
don't care at all."

Dustin stepped back. "You want me to act like a
jealous ass? I certainly could, but what would be the
use of that? I know that no matter what a man like
Catch does, you aren't going to follow just because
a kid with come-fuck-me eyes crooks his fingers at
you. You and I have been together for nearly twenty-five years. If you wanted to leave and follow a
young piece of tail, you would have. Same with me.
If I wanted someone else in my life, then I would
have gone out and found that." Dustin patted his ass
once again. "I don't. And every damned thing does
not have to be some sort of test."

"But it feels like it. After our talk, it's tilted everything on its side, and I'm not sure what I'm supposed to do." He left the bathroom and sat on the end
of the bed, thankful when Dustin sat next to him. "I
always thought I knew my role. I worked hard and
made sure the ranch was successful, and you always
looked after me and everyone on the ranch."

"And you still do that," Dustin told him. "You
always have. But I don't want you to ignore me
and take me for granted—any more than I should

take your hard work for granted." He leaned close enough that Marshall saw the deep azure flecks in Dustin's eyes. "We should appreciate each other and support each other. What do you want me to expect from you? That you'll do all the work on the ranch and that I'll just accept it and never give it another thought, even though it's what you do so well? If every ranch was run as well as you run ours, the beef industry would take over the planet." He drew even closer. "I know what it is that you do. I just want to be part of it."

Marshall leaned in those final inches. "You were always part of it. Every day we worked together was special."

"Yeah. But that was then. Do you see what we've become? We've slept in separate beds for years. We expected the other to just understand what we wanted without actually saying anything. And what's worse, neither of us questioned that for years. We thought it was just the way things were. You worked on the ranch during the day and worked long hours into the night on the books."

"Which I hate with a passion, by the way," Marshall interjected. "Sometimes the numbers swim so bad they make my head hurt and I have to do everything twice just to make sure I'm right."

Dustin's lips formed a straight line and his eyes hardened to cold steel. "You big, stubborn ass!"

"Huh?" Marshall hadn't expected that reaction at all. "Who's an ass? I do all that because I need to for the ranch and for us." He was fast going from mad to angry.

"Why didn't you fucking say so? I'm good at math, and in case you didn't know, I used to help my father with his books sometimes. The numbers swam for him too. Shit, Marshall, I can help you with those. You don't need to do it all yourself. The ranch is mine too." He shook his head, and Marshall put his hands to his forehead and fell back on the mattress.

"I think I have a headache," he moaned. "I've been doing that work all these years because I thought I had to, and…."

Dustin lay down next to him. "See? There are advantages to talking. I can take that task off your plate. You and I will need to work together so that I have the correct information to work from. Maybe we can get a new computer and set it up with a program specifically for herd management. And then we can transfer the books to a current software product that will do all the adding for us." He patted Marshall's hard belly. "It can be that simple."

"But how do we find this software?" That sort of stuff was over his head. He had put together a system that worked over the years, and then he'd just stuck with it. Sort of like his relationship with Dustin. He just kept doing the same thing, and now he found himself on the wrong path and being left behind. God, sometimes he just wanted things to be simple.

"I'll ask Winston. I'm sure he has something that he uses to manage his stock. Maybe we can find one system that will manage the rough stock as well, in case we decide to take that on. We can also talk to ranchers and folks we know at the rodeo. These events aren't just for fun. They're about networking. We can talk to people and find out what they use. It isn't like we're reinventing the wheel here. We already did that with the way we maintain our fields and the fact that we don't use pesticides or hormones and get the quality we do. That's where our advantage lies. Not in the computer program that's used to record it all. I'm sure we can figure something out." Dustin stretched.

"How come you make things sound so easy?" Marshall asked. "It can't be, and I know my system works. It has for twenty years."

Dustin shifted closer. "This is the same system that keeps you up late at night with numbers that swim before your eyes, and causes you to swear like a sailor?" Clearly he was enjoying this. "You and I will try together to find something that works. Besides, like it or not, I'm not you. If you want me to take over the books, then I can't just take your system and use it. That would work for you, maybe, but not for me."

Marshall could see that. "Is this the part where you tell me that I need to let go of some things if I want some help?"

Dustin chuckled. "I always knew you were a smart man." He glanced at the clock by the side of the bed. "We have half an hour until we need to meet in the lobby. I'm going to get unpacked and wash up. What about you?"

Marshall had closed his eyes and decided to try to relax and let go of the whole records issue. He knew Dustin was right, and damn, he'd be forever grateful if he didn't have to do that chore each evening. But giving up control was hard. It was part of how he took care of his family. "Okay. I'll be here." The bed was super comfortable, and he'd gotten up early to get chores done and make sure the men knew what to do while he was gone.

Dustin left the room, and Marshall heard the shower start. He was settled, and the room was otherwise quiet. A short nap would probably do him good.

But then a mental image of Dustin under the stream of water, the steam frosting the glass shower door with hints of Dustin's tanned skin glistening through, changed his mind. He climbed off the bed, pulled off his clothes, and slipped into the bathroom. He slid the shower door open enough to step inside.

"I thought you were napping," Dustin said as Marshall slid his arms around Dustin's still trim waist.

"I had a better idea," he whispered before sucking on Dustin's ear.

Dustin leaned back against Marshall's chest, and Marshall stroked his smooth skin, his cock settling right between Dustin's buttcheeks.

"I like it, but we really don't have a lot of time," Dustin moaned. "Oh damn, that's good." Dustin groaned softly as Marshall lightly pinched a nipple, sliding his other hand along Dustin's thick length.

"Are you sure?"

"Yes… no…." Dustin whimpered, and Marshall stroked him, knowing just the right pressure to make Dustin's leg shake. Damn, that was hot.

"How about *yes*. Let's go with yes. We have all the time in the world." He stroked harder, teasing the bud between his fingers, knowing the slight pain, combining with the pleasure, was nearly enough to overwhelm Dustin.

"Uh-huh," Dustin breathed as Marshall pressed him slightly forward, the water now cascading all down him.

Marshall picked up his pace. "I know what you like." He sucked Dustin's ear once again, continuing his sweet torture as Dustin began trembling in his arms. "That's it. I've got you, and I'm the one in charge of your pleasure. So stop fighting it and give it up. Let go for me." He picked up the pace still further, and Dustin's groan echoed off the tile like an opera singer at the height of an aria. Nothing sounded sweeter unless it was the gasp that preceded Dustin tumbling over the edge. To Marshall's ears there was no sweeter sound on earth.

Dustin leaned back against him, wrung out, breathing hard, while the shower washed away the evidence of his lover's pleasure. Marshall reached for the soap and lathered his hands, then washed Dustin clean. Then he held him, letting the water sluice over them before turning it off and grabbing the towels. Dustin sighed as he dried off, stepping out of the shower on legs that reminded Marshall of the unsteadiness of a newborn colt. He loved that he had done that to Dustin. "Do you think you can make it down to the lobby?" Marshall asked as they left the bathroom.

"I'm not that old," he groused, but the smile gave away the ruse completely. Marshall swatted his butt, and Dustin jumped away before stepping into his underwear and finally his jeans. He slipped into a yoked shirt and then threaded his belt through the loops.

"Is that…?" Marshall asked.

"You remember," Dustin said.

Marshall nodded. "How could I forget? That first rodeo. You took the bronc, and I nearly took the bull riding." He leaned closer. The buckle was simple, with a horse embossed on it. It hadn't been a fancy rodeo, not like the top-cut events they would both eventually top the leader boards in. But it was their first, and it held a special place in his memory. Judging by Dustin's choice to wear it, the memory still held for him as well.

"Come on. Get dressed so we can go." Dustin sat, and it was his turn to watch as Marshall dressed quickly. He wore only his regular buckle and stepped into his showing-off boots. Then he grabbed his wallet and keys while Dustin got the room card. They snagged their hats and headed for the elevator.

"Uncle Marshall," Noah said as they approached.

Marshall lifted Noah, then paused, turning to Anne. "The boys asked if they could call you that instead of the *mister*," Anne clarified with a smile. "I said I didn't think you'd mind."

"We're all cowboys," Oliver piped in, wearing his hat.

"Yup. You all ready to go?" Marshall said with a smile while Uncle Dustin took Oliver's hand, and they headed out into the heat. He called for the car, and they climbed in when it arrived. Once everyone was situated, Marshall pulled out and headed for the Stockyards. They probably could have walked, but he was concerned about Noah being out in the heat, and watching the cattle drive was probably going to be all the outdoor time they needed.

Parking didn't take long since Richard had a hang tag because of Noah, and once parked, they got out and walked toward the historic district, where people had already lined the street. "Let's head for the shady side."

"When will it start?" Oliver asked.

"In five minutes," Dustin answered him. "Let's stand here. The cattle are going to come from that way and then pass right in front of us. We have to stay behind the barricades." He put Oliver on his shoulders, and Marshall did the same with Noah.

Richard and Anne stood together, and eventually Richard's arm snaked around Anne's waist and she leaned slightly against him. It was good to see her relax a little. That made the entire trip worthwhile.

"I see 'em," Oliver said, pointing. He was so excited. Marshall knew that the cattle made this trip twice a day and they knew the route as well as the cowboys on horseback, who ostensibly kept them moving, though in truth they were there mostly for the safety of the onlookers. Still, it was quite a show as the cattle passed. "Ewww," Oliver said when one of the longhorns pooped.

"It happens. All cowboys learn to deal with it," Marshall told him, and that seemed to satisfy both boys. Besides, there were many more interesting things—like the mounted cowboys in red shirts, jeans, and chaps.

"They're cowboys like Uncle Dustin and you," Noah said more quietly, bouncing lightly on his shoulders.

Once the cattle had passed by, they headed down the street to the shopping area. Marshall lifted Noah down and carried him. The little guy had to see everything, and when they approached a Western-wear store, Marshall led the way inside.

"May I help you?" an older man asked as he approached.

"This guy needs a hat," Marshall said.

"Really?" Noah asked as Marshall set him down.

"Yup. You need a hat like Oliver." He helped Noah pick one out and made sure it had sizers that could be removed as Noah grew. Then he got both boys boots, and they left the store as happy as he remembered being when his daddy took him for his first pair of boots and bought him the hat that Oliver wore.

Richard walked next to him once they left. "How much…?"

Marshall shook his head. "Nothing. My daddy was a cowboy, and he got me my first hat and boots. I'm just passing it forward from one cowboy to the next." His throat grew scratchy and he turned away, because dammit, he was not going to get emotional on the fucking street.

"Daddy, can we get ice cream?" Oliver asked, pointing toward the shop across the street.

"We're going to eat dinner soon. Why don't we see if you have enough room afterward?" Clearly this was a practiced answer.

"Promise?" Oliver asked.

"Yes, I promise," Richard answered.

Marshall remembered that promises had meant a great deal when he was a kid. Too bad a lot of them had been broken and he'd learned not to rely on them.

"I promise too," Dustin told him, bumping his shoulder. "You can have ice cream after dinner." They wandered the area of town, occasionally passing costumed characters.

"Is he a real Indian?" Oliver asked.

"He is, and today we say Native American," Richard corrected.

"Red Bird?" Dustin asked, and the man in native dress turned toward them. "It is you. Dustin Meyers."

Recognition flashed on his face, along with a grin. "It's been too long," he said as they hugged. "Are these your boys?"

A cloud passed momentarily over Dustin's expression. "No. Marshall and I chose not to have children. This is Oliver and Noah, and their parents, Anne and Richard. Guys, this is Red Bird. Years ago we both were in the rodeo, and for a few years RB here was my traveling companion. We were barely eighteen at the time." Dustin smiled. "How have you been? I heard you got married."

"I did." His smile faltered. "My wife passed a few years ago. Cancer," he added softly.

"I have cancer," Noah chirped. "Oh, but I'm not supposed to talk about it because it makes Mommy and Daddy sad." He turned away, and Richard lifted his son into his arms and held him tight. Man, that took the wind out of the sails of that conversation.

"I'm sorry. I didn't know. How are the kids?"

"They're in college now. My oldest daughter is a junior and my son a freshman, both at A&M. My daughter is going to be a civil engineer, and my son is interested in agricultural economics. They're determined to return to the tribe and help make things better for everyone." He was clearly proud of both his children.

"Do you still fight cowboys?" Oliver asked.

Red Bird shook his head gently. "No. We made peace with the cowboys a long time ago. Now we just fight the government for our land rights. But we've been fighting for decades and will continue."

"How well I remember," Dustin said and hugged his friend once more before pulling a ranch card out of his pocket. "If you're in the area, stop by any time."

"I will." He hurried away.

Dustin turned to the others. "There's a steakhouse one block over. Let's go get some dinner. After the cattle drive, I'm ready for some beef not on the hoof." He led the way.

"Mommy, what's the gubament, and why is Mr. Red Bird fighting it? Doesn't he know fighting is wrong? Maybe the gubament could say sorry like you said I had to yesterday."

Marshall was glad he didn't have to answer that question, and let Anne figure out what to tell him.

"Mr. Meyers," the host at the restaurant said as they approached. "We heard you were in town and are so thrilled you're dining with us." He led them through the restaurant to a table that he had set up. "I saw you in Las Vegas the year you won the world championship. That was some amazing riding." He passed out the menus. "Your server will be with you in a moment." He flashed a smile and lingered for a second before hurrying off.

"Are you famous, Uncle Dustin?" Oliver asked.

Dustin shrugged.

"He's rodeo famous," Marshall whispered. "So we all have to be on our best behavior. Okay?" He winked, and Oliver sat straighter in his chair.

"I wanna be rodeo famous too someday."

"How about we get you a booster seat, our future rodeo star?" Richard asked.

Oliver shook his head. "Big boy rodeo cowboys don't need booster seats." He made it a pronouncement, and Anne turned away, trying not to laugh. Marshall and Dustin did the same, nearly failing to control their mirth, leaving poor Richard to deal with the issue itself.

"What does everyone want?" Marshall asked after clearing his throat, and they settled down to a Texas-sized dinner.

"THOSE BOYS are something else," Dustin said once they returned to the hotel room, full from

appetizers, steak, potatoes, and then ice cream like
Richard promised. Fortunately, the heat had abated
some once the sun went down, and after their ice
cream, both boys had fallen asleep in their parents'
arms and stayed that way the entire ride back to the
hotel.

"They're great kids." Marshall sat on the edge of
the bed. "That Oliver is so smart. The way he picks
up on things is astonishing." He got his boots off and
lay back on the covers, arms spread out like the entire bed was his.

"Yeah," Dustin agreed quietly, plopping into the
chair near the wall of windows. The room was high
up enough that the curtains were open, the lights
of the city spread out below. Marshall wondered
if Dustin was extra tired and figured it was best if
he got ready for bed. He stripped out of his clothes
and changed into a pair of light sleep pants, then sat
on the bed and turned on the television. Dustin was
still in the chair, staring out the windows. "If there
was something you could go back and change, what
would it be?"

Marshall shrugged. "I don't know. I think I'd try
to see where things got so hard between us and try
to put a stop to it. Maybe get you those stop-snoring
strips or just learn to ignore the sound and stay closer
to you." Because that had started them down the path
they were trying to get off of now. "Why this trip into
'what if' land?"

Dustin smiled. "It's nothing. Just me being stupid." He went into the bathroom and closed the door.
Marshall followed him with his gaze, wondering if it

was more than that. But the television caught his attention before Dustin came out, and he laughed at the antics of eleven-year-old Sheldon as Dustin emerged and joined him on the bed. Marshall took his hand, and they lay there side by side. When Dustin rolled over, pulling his hand away, Marshall shifted as well just so he could stay in contact with him, tamping down his nerves. Marshall wanted this weekend to go well, because he wanted to be part of this world again. He was just afraid that Dustin would say no.

Chapter 11

IT WAS amazing standing in the center of the arena the following evening after he was introduced, waving to the crowd as hundreds of camera flashes went off all at once. Dustin took the microphone that was handed to him and smiled, making sure the big screens got a good image of him. "This is a special event for me. Twenty-five years ago, I won the bronco riding events at this exact rodeo!" The crowd cheered. "It was my first ever all-around win." He held up the buckle he'd received that night. "Now it's time to pass the torch to the next generation of rodeo cowboys. Let's give them all a hand." Dustin stepped down and handed the microphone to the announcer, who proceeded to rev up the crowd as he introduced the cowboys in the first event.

Dustin carried his things out of the arena and then found his seat between Marshall and Oliver. Noah sat between his parents, and both boys jumped as the first gate opened and the evening's events began.

"Is he hurt?" Noah asked when the first rider hit the dirt. But he got up, waved his hat, and raced for the boards.

"He's okay. But riders *can* get hurt," Dustin told the boys. Then he pointed. "See over there? Those are people here just to help anyone if they do get hurt."

Oliver turned to him. "Did you get hurt?"

Dustin nodded. The truth, at least an abbreviated form of it, was probably warranted. "I did sometimes. And the people like them always helped me really fast. See, the bulls and horses are stronger than the men. That's why this is such a real challenge." He leaned closer. "Even when I got hurt, I still loved it, and so do these guys."

The next rider burst out of the chutes, and Dustin found himself clutching Marshall's arm as the bronc tossed the rider up and off his back in two seconds. He flipped through the air as the horse continued jumping and kicking. That was going to hurt. The clowns distracted the horse while others got to the rider. He got to his feet, and the crowd cheered, but Dustin knew the walk was only as far as the medical station. "There were times when I missed this... but it's for the young people now."

Marshall leaned right to his ear. "You and I are a little old for this event, but we can have our own private rodeo when we get back to the room." He practically vibrated with energy as the saddle bronc event continued. The boys were thrilled and practically jumped up and down every time the gate opened.

But for Dustin it was different. He had been good at what he did, and he'd loved the rodeo. He got to be the center of attention for a while, and he made good money. Dustin had also met Marshall at the rodeo, and they had such dreams. So he kept riding, training, and pushing because he wanted to do his part to make those dreams come true. And yes, he had taken chances when he was young in pursuit of those dreams. But now, as the gate opened and the bronc and rider burst onto the sandy arena floor, his nerves jangled, and he leaned forward, remembering those moments when he'd been up on one of those wild-ass crazy horses. God, he didn't want to do that again. This was a part of him that was better left in his youth. Dustin had grown up a lot since the days when he'd taken chances with his health and life.

"You okay?" Marshall asked.

Dustin nodded. "Yeah." He patted Marshall's hand and then stood and hurried up the stairs and out onto the arena concourse. He wasn't sure why this was bothering him so much. He'd been to rodeos before. Maybe he just needed to get his head on straight and breathe a little.

"Are you Dustin Meyers?" a man asked, holding the hand of a young boy. "Would you sign his program?"

"Of course." The man opened it to the page that had Dustin listed as the evening's special guest, and he signed the page. "You enjoying the rodeo?"

The kid nodded vigorously. "I want to ride the bulls when I grow up."

Dustin nodded. "I was too tall for the bulls. But you gotta do well in school too. There's a lot more to rodeo than just getting on the back of a horse or bull." He tipped his hat, and the kid looked at his father impatiently and started walking.

"Come on. We don't want to miss anything."

"Thanks for that," the father said. "He says all he wants to do is ride in the rodeo and that he doesn't need school for that." It was clearly a point of frustration.

"School and learning are a hell of a lot easier than any rodeo life. No matter how glamorous it may seem," Dustin said, tipping his hat once again before the man hurried to catch up with his son.

Dustin stopped at one of the food kiosks and grabbed some sodas, including two small Sprites for the boys, then headed back to their seats. He needed a reason for his sudden departure.

They barely noticed he was gone until he returned with the drinks. Anne thanked them, and the boys both grinned, thanking him when prompted lightly, their attention on the arena as they waited for the next rider.

"You missed an amazing ride," Marshall told him as Dustin sat down. "A local kid, wildcard slot, just rode the highest-rated bronc and made the eight with style. His score is going to be huge." He turned with a grin. "The ride of a lifetime."

"Sorry I missed it," Dustin said and waited as the next rider burst from the chutes. He sat back, reminding himself that he wasn't competing. There was no need for him to be anxious. But it was hard not to put himself in their places. He sipped his drink and did his best to let go and just watch. He didn't understand why this was even bothering him.

Once the last rider had competed and the standings were displayed for the first round, the energy in the arena seemed to shift into a higher gear. "What's going on?" Anne asked.

"This is a full rodeo, so they have a lot of different events, but it's also a top-cut event, so the best bull riders in the nation are here, and the fans are getting ready for the main event," Marshall explained, his excitement ratcheting upward. This was always Marshall's favorite, and it had the most fans of any of the rodeo events.

The arena cleared and a warning was issued before the lasers and fireworks lit up the arena. Fire burst from the floor as the riders were introduced to step forward to draw their bull. It was quite a production. Noah crawled into his mama's lap, and she held him. It was probably too much for him. Oliver stood, bouncing on his heels, and Dustin was grateful Marshall had gotten the front seats of the section.

"I always loved this," Marshall said and explained what was happening to the boys.

"They don't assign the bulls?" Richard asked.

"Nope. Each rider draws. That way no one can claim any bias. It's all random." Marshall pulled out the program, and the boys gathered around. "See, this is Hummer, the most difficult bull here. He's only been ridden once in fifty times. That means he's really hard to ride. So if the cowboy who gets him rides him for eight seconds, he's going to get a really good score. Now this one, Murcado, is the money bull. He's easier to ride, and you can get good style points and make a good score so you win some money." Dustin loved how Marshall was trying to make sure the boys understood.

"Come on, Money Bull," Noah said as though it were the bull's name.

"That's right. You can root for the riders or you can root for the bulls." Marshall motioned for the boys to come closer. "Since I'm a cowboy, I root for the riders."

Both boys looked so serious for a second. "Come on, *Money Bull* anyway." Noah was having fun, and Marshall lifted him into his lap. The little guy settled right there, and Oliver climbed into his daddy's lap.

"Do you want anything?" Dustin asked Anne.

She nodded slightly and slipped by them all, heading up the steps, probably for a few minutes by herself. Dustin wasn't sure how good a time she was having, but he admitted Anne was an amazing sport.

Of course, he found out how wrong he was once the riding started and Anne screamed for the riders as loudly as anyone else. It was always the quiet ones.

"THAT WAS awesome," Oliver said once the events for the evening were over. Noah was sound asleep in his daddy's arms, head resting on his shoulder. They waited their turn to get out of the arena, and when they reached the car, Anne and Richard got the boys into their seats. Noah didn't wake the entire time, while Oliver talked all the way back to the hotel about all the bulls and the horses and how he wanted to ride bulls and *whoo!*, every *whoo!* punctuated with his hands up like the riders did.

"Do you want to try mutton busting?" Anne asked him.

"Are you serious?" Richard asked.

Anne sighed as Dustin kept quiet. "Yes. If it's what he wants to do, then let's look into it." She sniffed. "As much as I want to, I can't wrap them in bubble wrap and stop them from getting hurt." Dustin turned and saw her lean against Richard. "Noah is getting stronger, and all I do is pray every day that the treatments have worked and that he's on the mend. I find myself taking his temperature three or four times a day just because I'm worried. And I can't live like that. He doesn't need that."

"Is Noah gonna die?" Oliver asked, throwing the words out there like a hand grenade and having no idea of their explosive power.

"No, honey," Anne said.

Dustin gave them privacy in back, but could imagine her checking on Noah to make sure he was asleep. At least that's what he would do. Dustin swallowed and closed his eyes, trying not to let his imagination pull up that old image of himself and Marshall that he'd put together years ago. It was a dream he had long ago given up on, but damned if that image didn't come forward, and every time, there was him, Marshall, and a child on a pony.

He and Marshall had talked about kids and decided against it years ago. Wishing that Marshall would change his mind or even bring up the topic now wasn't fair to either of them. Dustin didn't need the false hope, and Marshall deserved to have his wishes respected. Not that Dustin could blame

Marshall after the tough time he'd had, but some wishes seemed to hang on long after their expiration date.

THEY REACHED the hotel and got the kids out and the SUV in the hands of the valet. As they walked into the hotel, Noah woke and seemed to turn into the Energizer Bunny. Apparently a hungry bunny. They headed for the bar area and sat at the tables at the edge where they served snack food. While they were there, Marshall's phone chimed.

He answered it and wandered away to take the call. "How bad is it?" Dustin heard Marshall say, and Dustin groaned. "Okay…." Marshall turned away and stepped out of listening range.

"Thank you for bringing us, Uncle Dustin," Oliver said next to him.

"Did you really like it?" Dustin asked.

Both Oliver and Noah nodded. "Can we go tomorrow too?"

"I think Uncle Marshall and Uncle Dustin need to get back to their ranch so they can take care of the animals. That's the most important thing cowboys do. Now, once you two get your snack, you both need to go right up to bed, and then in the morning, your mom and I will take you to the pool so you can swim before we leave. Is that a deal?"

Dustin loved how both boys turned to each other and then nodded with huge grins.

"Here's your chicken nuggets, but let them cool a little before you eat them. Okay?"

The three of them sat with the boys as they ate, Dustin watching where Marshall stood outside, pacing slightly past the plate glass windows. Finally he nodded and some of the tension drained out of him. Whatever the problem was had either been solved or patched until they got home.

"Everything okay?" Anne asked Dustin as Marshall put his phone in his pocket and headed back inside.

"I think so." Dustin turned as Marshall sat down.

"We had a problem with Frenzy. One of the guys put him in the wrong corral, and he jumped the rails. They located him and got him back inside, and he's fine." Marshall shook his head. "He wasn't hurt, and I suppose they won't forget again."

Dustin could tell Marshall wasn't happy, and he had probably given whoever was responsible a talking-to and was now trying to calm himself down.

"Do we need to go back?" Anne asked.

"No," Dustin said firmly, not waiting for Marshall. "The guys have things under control, and it's good for them to take responsibility for things. Otherwise we'd have to manage everything, and then the ranch can't grow." He almost dared Marshall to disagree with him.

"That's true," Marshall agreed, and Dustin patted his leg under the table.

"Do you want anything? I ordered some guac and chips as well as artichoke dip. The boys are happy, and we all can have a beer if we want." He was thirsty, and they ordered a round and sat back. Even Marshall finally seemed to relax, and by the time their food came, the conversation was light and enjoyable.

Noah fell asleep in his chair, and Oliver played quietly with some trucks Anne had in her bag. It had been a while since Dustin spent an evening just talking without having to run out to feed the horses or clean up the kitchen. Ranch life never seemed to stop and just give them an hour where they could take a breath and relax. There was always something to do and something pressing on them.

"The doctors are hopeful that the treatments were successful," Anne was saying as Dustin pulled himself out of his own thoughts. "They said we were lucky because it was caught early." She set down her half-full mug. "But I don't think it matters. There's no phrase that I can think of that's worse than 'I'm sorry… your child has cancer.'"

"We've been fighting it with him for a year now."

"When will you know?" Dustin asked.

"A couple weeks. We'll bring him in to Children's in Dallas, and they'll do some more tests. Noah hates it because he gets poked. The poor thing has had so many needles put into him he has to feel like a pincushion. He used to cry when they did it early on, but now he just sits there."

"Noah wants a puppy," Richard interjected, probably to change the subject. "Actually, he asked me if we could get a dog just like Pal. I think he really has designs on your dog, and if he were older, he'd plan a caper to get him." He smiled.

Dustin laughed. "Pal is pretty amazing."

"We used to have more dogs on the ranch, but as they got older and started to pass away, it...." Marshall glanced at Dustin.

"I hated it. I got attached to each of them, so we didn't replace them." Dustin squeezed Marshall's thigh under the table. "I think it's time to get some more pups. Maybe we could see about rescuing a few dogs."

"That's a great idea," Richard said. "Maybe I'll take the boys and see if we can find a dog for them."

"Richard," Anne almost scolded. "Do you think that's a good idea?" She bit her lower lip. "You know who will have to take care of it." Yeah, most likely her.

"If you don't think it's a good idea, then we won't. But it would be good for the boys. We moved out of the city because we wanted Oliver and Noah to be able to have animals and other things that were impossible in that fourth-floor apartment. Why wait?" he asked, but the implication was pretty clear.

"I had a dog when I was Oliver's age. It was my job to feed him and make sure his water dish was full. Believe it or not, I used to get up at six o'clock before school to let him out every morning. It was part of my routine. Taught me responsibility."

"Was that Digby?" Marshall asked, and Dustin nodded. That dog had been amazing and his best friend.

"He was part of my life all through school and died just before I left him to join the rodeo. He was my playmate and the one I first came out to. For the record, Digby never spoke to me again." Anne and

Richard chuckled. Marshall groaned. "Okay… okay. No more bad jokes."

"How did you figure things out on that front?" Anne asked. "Growing up in Texas… that must have been rather difficult. I grew up in upstate New York, and I like to think it was easier. Everyone knew someone or had someone in their family who was gay." She shrugged.

"Other than Digby, I kept those feelings to myself until I met this one. Marshall pulled me out of my shell."

"I think we did that for each other," Marshall said. "Though your parents were a lot more accepting than mine."

"But things are good now. It was a lot tougher back then, though I don't want to say that it's a picnic for any kid who's different." Dustin turned to Richard. "I have to ask. Why here? Anne is a Yankee from New York." He flashed a teasing smile. "And you work from home, so you could live anywhere." Not that he didn't love Texas. It was home, and once it got into your blood, that was it.

"My parents lived outside Dallas, and I got a job here a while ago. I still work for the same company, but now I work from home all the time. They were going to need to get bigger office space."

Anne smiled. "And Richard convinced them that if they allowed some of their people to work from home, there would be no need for them to rent a larger office location. They could stay where they were, and the people working from home could share offices when they needed to come in. It was brilliant, to say the least, and they figure it saved them a lot of money, so they gave Richard a share of it." Damn, she was really proud of him.

"Mommy, I'm tired," Oliver said, and she lifted him onto her lap. Oliver curled right up and fell asleep in minutes.

"We're glad you decided to move in."

"We've been looking for a place in the country for a while. In the city, the boys had to be careful of everything. They couldn't even have bikes because of where we lived. Every kid should be able to have a bike. And we wanted to eventually get the boys a dog, but it would have to have been really small, and…." She shrugged. "The suburbs are danged expensive, and as you said, Richard could live anywhere. I'm hoping that I can work myself once the boys are in school."

"What do you do?"

"I was an accountant."

Dustin turned to Marshall with a grin. "Are you interested in working now?" Marshall asked. "We were just talking about the herd records and the ranch books."

Dustin snorted. "He's been staying up late for years doing them after the ranch work is done, and it's breaking his back. I'm okay with numbers and such, but if you wanted, you could take that over. Maybe start part-time." Marshall actually grinned and nodded. Dustin figured that once he thought about it, having someone else do the books sounded like a good idea. They should be able to swing that financially.

Anne glanced at Richard. "Is it something I can do at the house?" she asked.

Dustin laughed. "Yes. The first thing, though, is deciphering Marshall's system and getting it into a computer program. His method consists of spreadsheets, ledgers, Post-it notes, and enough cursing to turn the room blue. And that's just the books. The herd records are a completely different matter."

Marshall scoffed. "I'm not that bad. It's hard work for me, but I do it because it needs to be done."

"I can come over and see what you've got. Put together some systems and get you set up on basic programs that will make things easier. It would be nice to have something of my own to do."

Dustin stifled a yawn. "If you would, we'd both be grateful. Marshall and I are ranchers and cowboys. The books and financials are necessary. But…."

"I get that. We can get something set up, and if you want, then I can help out from the house. I still need to watch the boys while Richard works, but it would be something I could do at various times." She leaned against Richard. "Honey, we should get these boys upstairs and into bed. You know they're going to be up early because *someone* promised them that they could go swimming." Anne handed Oliver over to Richard before standing. She then placed her hand on Noah's forehead before lifting him gently into her arms. "Good night. And thank you again for everything. This has been a wonderful time."

The walked toward the elevator, and Marshall signaled the server and ordered another pair of beers. "Do you think that's wise?"

Marshall seemed to ignore Dustin for a second and then turned to him. "When was the last time we just had a beer?" Marshall leaned closer. "You complained that we don't spend time together...."

Dustin put his hands up. "It's just out of character. You maybe have one beer in the evening and then disappear into the office."

"Yeah, and I'm celebrating that we might have found someone to help us there."

"I thought you didn't like the idea."

Marshall shrugged. "The more I thought about it, the more I realized you were right. I'm trying to do everything to keep our ranch and our lives together, and I figure that if I freed up some of my time, then maybe if we decide to take on the rough stock...."

Dustin should have known. Here he had hoped that Marshall was agreeing to free himself up a little so they could have some time together, but it was just so he could make room for more work. Which wasn't going to fix their problems and would only make them worse. Nothing ever seemed to change. Marshall was always going to be so wound up in the ranch that whatever Dustin wanted wasn't even going to register on his radar screen because he didn't listen. Marshall had made some small efforts, but when it came to what was really important, he was always going to choose the ranch over Dustin, no matter what reasons he might give.

Their beers arrived, and Dustin downed his in a few gulps. "I'm going to go up to the room and get ready for bed." He placed the glass on the table in front of them and left, letting Marshall take care of the check. He heard Marshall call for him, but Dustin was tired and too angry to deal right now.

He saw Marshall striding his way as the elevator door slid open, but he got inside and let the doors close. He rode up to their floor and went right down to the room and inside. He actually thought of putting the hard lock on the door, thinking that maybe a night sleeping in the lobby would give Marshall a chance to pull his head out of his ass. But he wasn't going to be childish. Instead, he washed up and got undressed, turned out the lights, and slipped under the covers just as Marshall burst into the room.

"What the hell was that about?" Marshall demanded as he closed the door.

Dustin sighed. "I don't want to talk about it tonight. I'm tired, and it's been a long day." He rolled over toward the wall, listening as the bathroom door closed and the water ran. Then Marshall came out, switching off the light. Dustin didn't want to fight with him, but he was hurt, and lashing out seemed like a good idea in the moment, even if he regretted it now. His pride wasn't going to allow him to just give in, so he inhaled sharply as Marshall climbed into the bed.

He lay still, waiting to see if Marshall would say or do anything. Then there was movement behind him and a hand slid over his side and around his belly. "I don't know why you're so mad at me."

"I know," Dustin said with a sigh. "That's what's so damn frustrating."

Marshall's hand stilled. "What?"

Dustin rolled over. "It's pretty simple. The ranch is always going to be more important than me. I need to get used to that, I guess." He closed his eyes. "Nothing I do or want is going to be as important as working with the guys or buying that operation from Winston. You want that rough stock so bad you can taste it. I get that. But what I really want to know is if you want it more than you want me." Dustin rolled back over.

"Is this an either/or situation? Is that what you're saying? You really don't want to expand our business so we can be safer and more diversified?"

"Of course I want our business to be safe. But I also want a fucking partner who isn't working himself into the grave like my father did. Remember? He worked his ass off and dropped dead at fifty-two. I want a life, not just a ranch. You know, a life where maybe you and I can travel."

"We'll do a lot of traveling with the stock."

Dustin sighed. "I don't want rodeo travel. I want real travel where I can relax, sip a drink on the beach while waves roll in, and you and I have nothing to do. Maybe a trip to Italy to see the sights, or to castles in Germany. Traveling with the stock is work; it's not fun. Dammit, I want a little fun in my life. I think I've fucking earned it." He rolled back over.

"So… we won't get the rough stock and we'll continue doing what we're doing," Marshall said.

"I didn't say that. I just want some piece of you that isn't the ranch. That's mine."

"But I'm already yours," Marshall said as he scooted right up behind him. "You're the most important part of my life. You're my partner and my family."

"Marshall," Dustin said as levelly as he could, "the most important things in your life are the things you willingly spend your time with, and I'm sorry to say that isn't me."

Chapter 12

MARSHALL MULLED Dustin's words for much of the night and on the way home. What the hell did Dustin think was going on? The ranch was their business, and it provided their living. But maybe Dustin had a point.

Marshall took Richard, Anne, and the boys home before returning the SUV. Then he and Dustin drove out toward the ranch.

"What do you want me to do?" Marshall finally asked as they pulled out of the rental car office in his truck.

"Just spend some time with me. I know you really want to buy the rough stock operation, and you say that you want me to run it. But I know how it's going to happen. You'll decide how things are to be run, and over time you'll take over, and suddenly you'll be working from sunup to sundown in order to get everything done. It's what you do and who you are. But in that scenario, there isn't room for me."

"First thing, I meant what I said. You would run the rough stock operation." Marshall didn't see the issue. "I'm not going to muscle in on you."

"No. But will you *make time* for me? You'll be managing the cattle, I'll be running the rough stock, but what will we be doing together?" Dustin asked. "We'll never see each other. You do realize that this weekend is the most time you and I have spent together in years. And it's not that I don't appreciate it—I do. But let me guess. We'll get back to the ranch, and before you can say 'cow shit,' you'll be off to see what's going on, and I'll go to the barn or somewhere else, and…."

Marshall sighed. "Okay. What do you want to do?"

"Excuse me?"

"We've been gone two days. There's going to be a number of things that we need to check on."

"Such as?" Dustin asked. "We have good men who are more than capable of watching the ranch for a day and doing their work. Why is it necessary to check over everything? We can talk to them, find out what was and wasn't done. Then we can finish the chores and let that be the end of the day. Why look for more work than is necessary?"

It was part of Marshall's nature to trust no one when things were important. Patrick and Willy knew the ranch backward and forward, though, and they were capable of leading the rest of the men. Dustin knew he could trust them.

"Okay. Maybe you have a point," Marshall said and actually smiled before pulling into the ranch and parking in his usual parking space.

"How was the rodeo?" Patrick asked as they got out.

"It was great. There were some amazing rides. The boys had a lot of fun," Marshall answered as he looked around. "What happened here?"

"Other than our excitement with the devil horse, it was quiet. We got the list of chores done, and I got Jackson started on the stalls for tomorrow."

Marshall smiled. "Good work. Thanks for taking care of everything. Where are the guys now?"

"Just finishing up," Patrick said. "The cattle are in a good place right now with plenty of readily available water, and with the rain, the fields are still growing really well. I did the estimates of feed we'll need for the rest of the summer, and it's really good." He seemed proud, and Marshall looked it over.

"Great work," Dustin said, and Marshall let his gaze slide to him. God, he was stunning in his jeans and simple shirt. Why hadn't he taken the time to really appreciate him before?

"Yes. Really good. Tell the guys that once the chores are done, they can knock off for the day. Is there anything you need me or Dustin for? If not, then he and I have a few errands we need to run, so we'll be gone for the better part of the day." If Dustin was right and he had been ignoring him, then he needed to do something about it. On a lot of ranches, Sundays were the rest day for the family. Marshall had never really thought that way. There had always been too much to do, especially when they were starting out. Maybe Dustin was right, and his ruts were so deep it was hard to change.

"Everything is good," Patrick told him. "I'm going to finish up, and I'll let the men know. Thanks."

He hurried off, and Marshall went inside with Dustin. Pal greeted them enthusiastically, and they let him outside. That dog did his business fast and was right back inside, soaking up all the attention they had to give him.

Then Marshall sat watching Dustin, and Dustin watched him. When in the hell did it get so hard? The longer they squatted, petting Pal, who was in complete doggie heaven, Dustin staring at Marshall expectantly, the heavier their silence grew. What the fuck was he supposed to do? Come up with some scintillating topic to talk about or figure out something for them to occupy the evening? This was why he worked all the time. Then he didn't have to try to figure out what to do next, or where to go next, or what to eat next. All that shit was taken care of with work. It made life so much easier. But his work wasn't good enough anymore. Blood, sweat, and tears didn't account for shit, it seemed like. Now resentment started to take root.

"I was thinking…," Dustin began, and Marshall blew out his breath before his head exploded. "Maybe you and I could go into town for dinner and see a movie."

"You mean like a date?" Marshall asked.

Dustin shrugged. "If you don't want to…." He lowered his gaze. "How about this. You go on out there and see what's going on with the guys. You're itchy and jumpy to do it. Check the place out and make sure all is right with the world, but you be back here by five. I'll cook us a nice dinner, just for you and me. And then we'll stay in, watch a video, and neck like teenagers in the back row of the theater. Oh, and we'll lock all the damned doors."

Marshall got to his feet. "That's a deal." He waited for Dustin to stand and then kissed him hard, tugging him close. "That's just a taste for later." Then he was out the door so he could hop on an ATV to check out his domain.

MARSHALL KNEW he was late. He checked his watch for the third time as he opened up the ATV and took off toward the ranch. It was five minutes till five, and he had promised Dustin he'd be home. But dang it, time had almost gotten completely away from him. He thought about calling, but he just wanted to get back.

Marshall opened up the throttle, going as fast as he dared. This was his land, and he knew every bump and rise in it. He checked his watch again as he continued home. The building came into view. Marshall was sure that Dustin could hear the engine and would know he was close by. After pulling directly into the equipment shed, he unloaded his tools and put them away. Then he strode across the yard toward Pal. The dog was always eager to greet them when they got back from anywhere, but this time he stayed in the grass like he was guarding something.

"Dustin?" he called, poking his head into the house.

"Yeah," Dustin answered from inside, footsteps approaching.

"Come out here a minute," he said and waited. "The dog's acting funny." He led Dustin around to where Pal was still in the grass. Pal lifted his head as they approached and growled at them. "That's enough," Marshall snapped, and Pal stopped.

"Puppies," Dustin said. "He's guarding puppies." He squatted down. "Marshall, go get some milk in a bowl. We need to see if these guys are big enough to eat on their own."

Marshall hurried away, and by the time he returned, Dustin was cradling three pups in his arms. "How bad is it?"

"Their eyes are open and they're squirming like crazy." Dustin set them down, and they bounded through the grass to the bowl and began drinking like they were starved. He turned to Marshall. "Someone dumped these pups out there. They sure aren't country dogs. The pups are so small, and yet they seem to be about four or five weeks old, judging by how they're acting."

Dustin pulled out his phone and called the vet. "Darren, need a favor. Pal found some puppies and has been guarding them. They're drinking milk right now, but we aren't sure how old they are. The things are so small."

"I'm out at a call a couple miles from your place. I'll stop by on my way home. Gotta go." He hung up, and Marshall relayed the message. "They're still hungry." Marshall took the bowl inside and poured some more milk in it. Then he added some of Pal's food and mashed it up, creating a light porridge. Hopefully it would be easy enough for them to digest. He set the bowl near the puppies, and they ate again.

Marshall sat back, snapping his fingers. Pal hurried over, and Marshall stroked his head. "You did good. Are there more? Daddy has these pups. Are there more? Where did you find them?" Of course, Pal didn't react. "Are there more pups?" Marshall asked with more excitement and stood up. "Show me where you found them?" Marshall watched as Pal kept looking toward the barn. He went in that direction, and Pal hurried past him and around the side. Marshall stepped carefully as Pal jumped through the grass and stopped near an indentation. Another pup squirmed on the ground, and Marshall lifted it into his arms. "You're such a good boy." He checked for others and then hurried back to Dustin. The food wasn't entirely gone, and he lifted the bowl and let the newest addition eat what was left.

"Someone dumped them, all right. There was what was left of a box beside the barn. I think Pal tore it apart to get to them." Pal nosed around the puppies before lying in the grass, looking for all the world like a proud papa.

"He always was a good boy," Dustin said. "I wonder what kind of dogs they are. Way too small to be ranch pups." The little guys weren't much bigger than Marshall's hands, even now.

The vet pulled into the drive and joined them in the grass, the pups curling into a pile in the shade. "What do we have here?" He bent down, peering at the puppies. Pal moved closer, sitting so he could preside over the proceedings. The vet lifted one and then each of the others. "Looks like you have three boys and a little girl. They seem a little emaciated, but regular food will take care of that. Otherwise, they're healthy enough. We'll need to deworm them, and I want to take some blood and stool samples just to be sure. I'll leave a flea treatment for each of them because they're infested, poor things. Call the office and we can schedule their shots."

"What kind of dogs are they?"

"I'd say they're terriers. They have that look, and the color is right. I mean, look at the sort of mottled blond coats with the black around the muzzles. They might be cairn terriers. Why would someone dump dogs like these?" he asked himself. "I can't be sure, but these pups will grow into beautiful little dogs. About twenty pounds or so, and their color is gorgeous." He lifted one of the pups again, the little guy squirming in his hand. "I just don't get it. I mean, they're not that old, but they look like perfect terrier puppies."

"Okay." Marshall had hoped that maybe they were just young and that he had found dogs that he could use on the ranch. But no such luck. "What do we do with them?"

"We'll raise them and figure it out," Dustin said, but Marshall knew better.

"They're small hunting dogs. They were originally bred to hunt vermin. Now we use them as pets, but they're intensely loyal and fearless. These pups will defend the ranch against all foes, no matter the size." He smiled, and Marshall could see the look in Dustin's eyes. *Find them homes? No way.* He could already almost feel his partner's heart wrapping around each of those puppies. It was going to be hard to get him to give up any of them, and it seemed that Pal had adopted them as well.

"Sure are pretty," Marshall said, lifting up one of them. "Look at that face."

"Bring them into the office in the next couple of weeks and we'll get them started on their shots. Let me leave you the flea treatment. It's especially for puppies. Give them a flea bath first thing and then feed them the pills. I'll leave some puppy-specific shampoo for you to use on them as well as some puppy food. They're going to want to eat a lot, I suspect, but that isn't going to hurt them. I'd be concerned if they didn't." He stood and went to his truck, then returned with the supplies.

"Thanks for coming out. They can't have been there long."

"They definitely weren't." He smiled. "Take good care of them, and call me if you need anything and to make appointments for their shots. I'll keep an ear out in case I hear anything." He shook both their hands and then got into his truck and left.

Dustin took the supplies inside and returned, lifting two of the pups. Marshall took the other two, and they went right into the bathroom, ran warm water in the tub, and gently bathed the pups. Pal stood by the door, watching while they each took two pups. Once the pups had been rinsed, Dustin and Marshall dried them off and wrapped them in towels. After they were dry, Dustin gave them each the pill for fleas, then made a bed in the mudroom.

"We're going to need to fence them in somehow, or they'll run all over the house leaving us presents until we get them trained to go outdoors," Marshall said. He went in search of something they could use.

"I hear Pal found some puppies?" Jackson said as Marshall was heading toward his truck.

"Yeah." He couldn't help smiling. It had been a while since they had puppies in the house. "Gotta find something to keep them from peeing all over the house."

Jackson hesitated and then turned to his truck. "I got one of those baby gates in the back. My mom used it for my sister and me and had me haul it out with some junk the other day." He rummaged in the back and pulled out the wood-and-plastic contraption. "Will this work?"

"Yeah—thanks." Marshall took the gate and waved as Jackson pulled out of the yard.

"Where did you get that?" Dustin asked when he returned inside.

"Jackson had it in the back of his truck with some stuff his mom wanted him to get rid of." Marshall put the gate across the mud room entrance after Dustin locked the outside door, set up some bedding, and laid out newspapers. Once the puppies were in their new home, they romped a little before settling down in their bed.

"Well, that wasn't how I expected to spend the evening," Dustin said. "Thank you for your help."

"What are we going to do with all of them?" Marshall asked. "And please don't say that we're going to keep them all. Two can stay, and we'll need to find homes for the other two. Okay?" Marshall liked having dogs on the ranch, but they didn't need four terriers.

"I agree to that." Dustin stood. "Why don't you go get cleaned up and I'll go make us some dinner." He patted Marshall on the shoulder. Marshall wanted to grab him and yank him close, but he was a mess after the water that had splashed on him combined with the dust from being outside. So basically, parts of him were caked with mud that he really needed to get off.

Marshall took his shower and put on comfortable clothes. The scent of dinner called him as soon as he opened the door. It drew him to the kitchen, where Dustin had put two small steaks on. "I'm finishing the potatoes in the oven, and I have some fresh green beans. The table is set, so if you want to sit down, I'll have things ready to go in ten minutes."

"Do you want some help?" Marshall asked. He put on some music and slipped his arms around Dustin's waist.

"You know that isn't helping." Dustin turned, and Marshall swayed them both to the music. "I need to finish cooking."

"Come on." Marshall turned him around and pulled Dustin into his arms, moving them to the music. It had been a long time since they'd danced together. "Just for a few seconds." He swung Dustin around, and his cowboy went right along with it. Dustin had always had rhythm, and it showed on the dance floor and in other places as well.

"I need to make sure your dinner doesn't burn," he sang in tune to the radio and then backed away. "Sometimes you're such a goof. I think that's why I fell in love with you in the first place." Dustin went right back to the stove to check the meat and beans before pronouncing them done. He made up their plates and brought them to the table, while Marshall got a couple bottles of beer from the refrigerator, opened them, and placed one at each setting.

"Where's Pal?" Marshall asked, looking around. He usually lay under the table at dinner, hoping a choice morsel would fall into his domain.

"With the pups. He's lying just outside the gate, watching them," Dustin said. "He's been doing that since we put them in there."

"We're going to need to get them active after dinner or they are going to be up all night." Marshall took a bite of the steak, humming softly. It was amazing, as Dustin's dinners usually were. "You always take such care with your food. How do you do that?"

"It's something I just learned. Mom was a good cook, but Dad always believed that women belonged in the kitchen. Or at least that his son didn't. I never really got to learn much from her. But once I was on my own, I used to call Mom for her recipes and things, and she helped me learn over the phone. She always told me that spice didn't mean making something hot but was about adding flavor. She also told me to taste what I'm making, because if I didn't like it, nobody else was going to either." He smiled as he ate, and they grew quiet. "What's on your mind?"

"Nothing important. Just thinking about when you and I met. God, we danced around each other for a while, and then you finally got up the nerve to kiss me... and from there it was like fireworks."

Dustin chuckled. "I was so scared for such a long time before that."

"You were scared? I had already been kicked out of my family, and I was so afraid that if I made a move, you'd hate me because I hated myself. But then you kept watching me, and I was watching you."

"It's the dance," Dustin said. "Everybody does it. Looks across the room, those first words, maybe even a light touch, and then that first date or the time you first open up to someone. It's all a dance, and the two of us both had two left feet. You remember?"

"Do I! We seemed to send each other the wrong signals for weeks. I couldn't quite figure out how to let you know I liked you without alerting all the guys that I did." He shook his head. Those had been such different times. Marshall had been so filled with shame and self-loathing, lashing out at everyone.

"You remember the time you tried to punch the bull after it threw you?" Dustin teased.

"They almost suspended me for it. But one of my friends convinced them it was the fall that had disoriented me for a while. God, I was wild and nuts back then. You, on the other hand, were steady and almost calculating. I remember watching you watch the other riders, studying them and the horses. You knew how they behaved and reacted so when you had to ride them, you had a plan. I was impressed and jealous because I could never do that. I just had to go with it." Marshall ate his potatoes, thinking of how out of control he'd been... and how damned lucky he hadn't done anything really stupid.

"Yeah. That was the anger and pain," Dustin said softly. "You were a real bad boy back then." He finished his steak and potatoes. "I first saw you and wondered about you. I was scared shitless because I wanted to be normal, and yet I took one look at you and knew I needed to figure out how to talk to you. But what if you didn't like me?" He shook his head. "I must have stayed away from you for weeks, too attracted to just walk away and too scared to make a move. Then, to my surprise, you made one."

Marshall chuckled. "And we almost got caught. Scared both of us."

"Yeah. But it didn't put you off. We got more careful, and you got more horny." Dustin continued eating, and Marshall made a honking sound. It was a cheesy joke, but Dustin laughed anyway. "Things seemed so importantly complex then, and yet when I look back on it, it was really so simple. We were taking care of ourselves, and all we had to do was ride and get to the next event on time."

Marshall sighed. "And stop ourselves from getting drunk enough that we couldn't ride or drive."

"That was never my problem. Or yours, as I remember." Dustin finished his dinner and set his plate aside.

"I think if I hadn't met you, I probably would have developed a drinking problem. I was so angry and wound-up that I had been drinking a lot. But then I had something much better to do, and you didn't drink, so I didn't either." Marshall set down his fork and put his plate next to Dustin's. "You always were a good influence on me." He took Dustin's hand. "A lot of things are different now."

"They have to be. We aren't kids anymore, and we've built a life here. It's something that has to be maintained and nurtured. We've worked too hard for the things we've built to fall apart. Back when we were kids, we had nothing to lose."

"Or at least it felt that way. We told ourselves that it was the other guys who got injured. That it wouldn't happen to us. Oh, we both had injuries, but nothing serious. It was the other riders who got trampled. We were too smart for that and knew how to get out of the way. We had nothing to lose... but our lives, but we didn't think about it." And now it seemed that was all Marshall could think about. They had a thriving ranch that provided for him, Dustin, and all the people on it. But Marshall had seen how quickly things could spiral out of control and crash right down to nothing. And he was determined that wouldn't happen to them.

"I know all that. Like I said, things are different now."

"Yeah, and we're old enough to start looking in the rearview mirror and wonder what's coming up on us." Dustin stood. "I'm not saying that you and I shouldn't be vigilant or that we shouldn't work hard. But do you remember the other half of that equation?"

Marshall followed Dustin with his gaze as he drew closer.

"We used to play hard too. But the playing part seems to have vanished a long time ago. It's started to make a reappearance now, and I want to make sure it becomes a regular part of our lives again." Dustin rested his hands on Marshall's shoulders, the heat sinking under his shirt. "Do you remember how you used to make furniture, like the headboard in our room? The coffee table in the living room that you gave me for Christmas the year we bought this place?" Marshall could feel Dustin leaning closer, the heat around him intensifying. He didn't even need to see it.

Marshall swallowed hard. "And you used to draw. I remember some of the ones you did. There's the bucking bronc framed in our bedroom." His voice was rough and his throat dry. It didn't matter how many times he swallowed; it stayed that way. Marshall remembered Dustin giving him the bronc drawing for that same Christmas. There was so much of their history in this house and this place.

"We need to do those things again. It doesn't have to be all the time, but we enjoyed them, and we can again. Maybe if we rediscover what we liked about ourselves, we can figure out what we had in each other." Dustin came around and Marshall got to his feet, encasing Dustin in his arms.

"I know what we have, and I intend to remind you of it… fully… for at least the next few hours."

The pups began to whine, and Pal barked. Dustin put his head on Marshall's shoulder, both of them groaning softly. "Let's go feed them and take them outside so they can run around."

Dustin made up some food with milk to make it easier for the pups to digest and set it down behind the fence. The four pups made a mad scramble for the food, even stepping into the pan in order to get to it. They ate as though they were starving, and it occurred to Marshall that they probably had been for a while, and that made them all a little more desperate. Marshall wished they had the mother of the pups so she could calm them, but that wasn't possible, so they did their best, with Pal overseeing everything.

Once the food was gone and their little puppy bellies distended slightly, Marshall lifted each pup, wiped it off, and handed it to Dustin. Once all four had been cleaned, they carried them out to the front lawn, where the pups romped and played with Pal, some of the guys coming over to join in on their way out.

"What are you going to do with them?" Patrick asked, lifting one of the adorable little bundles of fur.

"We're keeping two of them," Dustin pronounced. "And I think one of them is going to be for Noah and Oliver. So there will be one pup that we'll need to find a home for."

All the guys looked at each other, and half of them said they wanted the little guy. "Okay. What we'll do is put the names of everyone interested into a hat, and we'll draw a winner. Not going to happen for a couple weeks, so no staking a claim. Dustin gets first pick, and then the boys will choose. Is that clear? Good." Marshall grinned. "Until then, we're using the front door because the pups will be in the mudroom. Take off your boots before coming in that way."

The pups began to settle in the grass, so they lifted them and carried the little ones inside. They had done their business and were praised for going outside. Once the pups were in their area, they settled right down, with Pal lying outside to keep watch. Pal got his share of praise as well before Dustin turned to Marshall.

"Well, it seems it's Sunday. Delta's with her family. The guys are heading to town for a little fun. Patrick promised that he wouldn't let anyone stay out too late. So you and I have the house all to ourselves. Whatever will we do?"

Marshall lunged, propelling Dustin down the hall even as he pulled at his shirt. "I think I've been cockblocked by the ranch, horses, dogs, cattle, and now puppies. So I say strike while the iron is hot, and mine is on fucking fire." Marshall knew he was growling, but he didn't really care. All he wanted was Dustin under his hands and on that damned bed.

It seemed Dustin had the exact same idea, as he efficiently got Marshall out of most of his clothes before they tumbled onto the mattress together, lips never parting from their reinforcing cycle of desire.

God, he loved getting his hands—and the rest of him—on Dustin. He had hoped that they would have a chance to reconnect this weekend, and things hadn't quite worked out the way he had expected on that front.

"Everything seems to get in the way lately," Dustin told him between intense kisses. Marshall was glad that the door was closed and that his phone was in the other room. Short of a fire somewhere on the property, anything that arose on the ranch could most definitely wait.

"I think it's been that way for far too long." He managed to get Dustin's pants shimmied down below his hips. His own hung on his legs. He lowered his jeans and kicked them to the side. Marshall was determined, and soon enough he got them naked and Dustin positioned up on the bed with his head on the pillow. "This is going to be fast."

"Oh God, yes," Dustin moaned, and they both reached for the nightstand. Marshall came up with the lube and slicked his fingers. He slid them into Dustin with a moan each. Damn, he was tight, and Marshall used plenty of slick before positioning himself and pressing forward.

Instinct took over, and it required nearly all his control to pause for Dustin's sake before he drove into him. Marshall rolled his hips, leaning over Dustin, drawing him upward in a deep kiss as he continued his movements. No one had ever made him lose control the way Dustin did. Not that Marshall had much experience in that area. Before Dustin, the few encounters he'd had had been furtive ones that left him unsatisfied and feeling dirty. They only added to his shame. Dustin had ended all that, and as Marshall looked into those deep blue eyes, he knew why he had to fight for this man. Without Dustin, Marshall wasn't complete. He had long ago given Dustin a part of his body, heart, and soul, and he was never going to get them back, no matter what he did.

"Marshall," Dustin called, quivering from head to foot. Marshall tugged at Dustin's lower lip with his, pulling slightly and then renewing the kiss as soon as Dustin's lip sprang free. He wound his arms around Dustin, holding him tighter as he continued shimmying his hips, Dustin shaking and whimpering.

"That's it. Just let go," he whispered. "That's all I want. Let me see you completely lose it for me." God, there was nothing sexier, hotter than Dustin when he completely lost control, and Marshall pushed Dustin higher, feeling in his breath and his shaking muscles that he was about to shatter. And when he did, Marshall was going to be right here, holding him, ready to catch him so he didn't fall. And damned if, just like that, Dustin didn't open his mouth wide as his release washed over him. It was a gorgeous sight, one that sent Marshall careening into his own release, holding Dustin tight.

MAN, HE was getting old if it took him so long to open his eyes after making love. Marshall slowly cracked his eyelids open, wondering just how long the two of them had lain still, just breathing and holding each other. Their bodies had separated, and still neither had moved. Marshall lifted himself and managed to lie on the mattress next to Dustin, still holding him close but not finding the energy to do anything else other than breathe.

Dustin nestled in closely and laid his head on Marshall's arm. "You were always damned good at that," Dustin whispered.

"Yeah…." Marshall felt himself preening a little. Well, as long as he could preen with his voice or maybe a smile, because he wasn't moving for any reason. "We were always in tune that way."

"That's for sure. There were never any problems in the bedroom… until we didn't sleep in the same bed." There was no heat in his words, but Marshall felt it anyway.

"As I remember, you snored loud enough to wake the dead," Marshall teased. "It's a miracle the house isn't haunted with the spirit of every dog we've ever had that's buried in our little pet ceme- tery out back." He chuckled.

"Yet you've been sleeping in here with me for weeks." Even though Marshall couldn't see it, he knew Dustin was smiling. There was just something in his voice.

"You don't snore any longer. What happened, anyway?" Marshall asked. "I mean, you always snored. Did you give it up for Lent or something?" His mama raised him Catholic, so every year he had to do without something. The thing was, his mama used to decide what he had to give up, and usually it never returned on Easter.

"No. I think things changed as I got older. It hap- pens, I guess," Dustin answered. "But we didn't, not for a long time." He shifted even closer.

"I'm trying," Marshall said, even though a lot of the time, he wasn't sure what he was supposed to be trying to do.

"We both are. Things don't fix themselves over- night. But we're closer than we have been in a while, and that's good." Dustin closed his eyes again, and the conversation faltered. Not that it concerned

Marshall. It seemed that for quite a while, they filled the time together with talk. Being alone together—and silent—told him that they were truly comfortable with each other, and Marshall liked that. They'd taken a step forward. Now… somehow… they had to figure out how to make it the rest of the way.

Chapter 13

DELTA HAD made breakfast, and Dustin sat at the table across from Marshall, yawning and bleary-eyed. She set a mug in front of him, and Dustin thanked her. It was taking him some time to get used to his new routine. Usually he would make breakfast and fill his day with inside chores. For the past few weeks, he'd been working more on the ranch and helping Anne merge their records into the new computer system. He wasn't sure which was more taxing, and his body needed a little time to adjust. Delta did an amazing job keeping the house clean, and Dustin didn't miss that chore at all, but not cooking was something he was still getting used to. Over the years it had become something he really enjoyed.

Marshall set down his empty mug. "We're heading out to scan the north section for invasive plants that can hurt the cattle. Looks cloudy this morning, and it might rain this afternoon, God willing." It had been dry for the past few weeks, so rain would be welcome.

"Okay. Sorry I'm a little slow this morning," Dustin said. He sucked down his tea. Marshall, on the other hand, was as full of energy as a cheerleader at a high school football game. Hell, Dustin might have to tell him to calm his perky ass down. "What has you so raring to go?"

Marshall pulled out the chair across from him. "Winston called half an hour ago, and things have changed." His expression darkened. "It seems he has cancer, and it's pretty bad. He said the doctors were optimistic, but that if he can beat this thing, he's not going to have the energy to go on running his ranch, and he wanted to meet with us to see if we might be willing to take over his operation." His tone was heavy and serious even as his body thrummed with energy.

"Okay," Dustin said levelly. "We've talked about this, and I've had a chance to think about it and get my head around it. You really want to do this, I know, and you want me to run the operation." Which, frankly, Dustin thought he'd be good at. He knew rodeo horses, and Marshall knew the bulls. "I have a million questions, and since you already talked to me about this, I made a list. I'll warn you, it's pretty long, and we have to finish this transition of our books before we can give a final answer." He wasn't going to make an important decision like this with only part of the information they'd need. "As you said, we've spent a lot of our blood, sweat, and tears in this place. I'm not going to endanger that. I won't."

Marshall nodded slowly. "I won't either." There was a touch of hurt behind his avowal, though.

"Marshall," he said cautiously, "I'm not saying no, but we can't throw caution to the wind. We have to make a sound decision. When does Winston want to meet with us?"

"He said next week, once he gets back from the hospital in Dallas." That seemed to take some of the wind out of Marshall's sails. "And I agree with you. We need to do this right. I know I'm excited about the possibility, and if we're going to do this sort of thing, we need to do it now before we can't do it any longer."

"That's no reason to do anything." Dustin tried to keep the frustration out of his voice, but still he narrowed his gaze. "Is that why you want to do this? Because you're afraid of getting older? You want to try to recapture your rodeo days by running the rough stock and going to the rodeo, being part of the thrill?" He sat back. "We aren't children any longer. This is our home, and I won't put it in danger or allow you to do that either. Not on some rodeo cowboy midlife crisis." Maybe that was the answer to all of this. Hell, it was possible that they were both going through some sort of midlife shit, with both of them craving what they thought they'd lost. Except Dustin just wanted things with Marshall to be the way they were. Maybe Marshall wanted to recapture his youth somehow, and he thought this business with Winston was going to get him that. It wasn't going to, because as much as they might want to be able to turn back the clock, life marched in only one direction, and that was the way it was.

"Bastard," Marshall swore under his breath. "You should know me better than that."

Dustin wasn't going to back down on this. "Yes, I should. But the way you look when you talk about it, and the way you think traveling with the bulls is going to be so much fucking fun? It's work, a ton of it, as you should be well aware." He took a deep breath, but he'd be damned if he was going to keep quiet. "I have to know that you're taking this as seriously as a heart attack." Because Dustin was. This was a huge commitment, not something to be taken lightly.

"I am," Marshall gritted out between his teeth. "And I know this is going to be good for us. We have a world-class beef operation. This will diversify us and make things easier for Winston, knowing his operation is in good hands."

"Or it could sink us. We're cattle men. We have been for twenty years. It's our business and what we truly know. Yes, you and I rode in the rodeo, but we didn't take care of the horses or the bulls. They had their own handlers. What if we take this on and the men at Winston's don't want to work for a gay couple? Suddenly we have animals we don't know how to care for and no one to help us. Did you think of that?"

"You're scared," Marshall said flatly.

"Damn right I'm scared. I know to you that seems like weakness, but it's not. Fear keeps you on your toes, and if we do this, we are going to talk about every goddamned detail until this fear goes away. We'll have a plan for the finances, what we're

going to do with the additional land, how we'll manage the people, everything. And we'll have contin-
gencies too." Maybe it was the fear, but he wasn't
going to give up on any of this. "And we're going
to have a plan on how we'll manage our own time,
because I'll be damned if I'm going to let us get so
buried in the work that we forget about each other
again." That was what he was really afraid of.

"First thing, I don't see you and me traveling
to any rodeos we don't want to go to. We'll have
a trusted road team with people the bulls and horses know. Secondly, we'll need to enfold Winston's
operation into ours. At first I suppose we'll need to
operate both places, but over time we can centralize
things here. I've already drawn up plans based on
the stock that Winston has, and he agreed that he'd
still like to be involved if he's able. We would need
to talk to the men that Winston has and see what they
think too." Marshall really seemed to have thought
this through. "And yes, we need to make sure that
the finances work out. But we've been saving up
capital for the past five years so we would be able to
do something like this. That's part of why I've been
working so damned hard. I was trying to save us the
cost of another ranch hand so we could bank that
money and be able to make an investment to allow
the operation to grow." Marshall seemed so earnest,
and Dustin didn't mean to throw cold water on his
ideas. "I know it's faster than I thought it would be,
but let's see about getting the financial information
together and going over the information that Winston has. We can go from there."

Dustin felt a small piece of his worry slip away.
"Okay. Then we'll do our homework before we jump
into this." He still wasn't sure about Marshall's moti-
vations for this venture, but he'd take that.

"Yes." Marshall tapped the table as though the
deal was done and then stood. "You coming?" He
checked his phone. "A section of fence went down."
Marshall replied to the message. "You want to handle it with me?"

"Sure. Give me five." Dustin finished his coffee
and quickly ate the eggs and sausage that Delta had
for him. "Thanks," he told Delta before heading out
of the house, striding to where Marshall was already
loading the equipment in the truck. "Where are we
headed?"

"Very north of the property against that open
wooded area. We need to keep the cattle out of there
or we'll never find them." He jumped in the truck
and revved the engine. Once Dustin got in, he barreled out the way he always drove. Dustin kept quiet,
looking as they turned just past Richard and Anne's
house. A little up the side road, Marshall turned left
once again, and they followed an old access road
that was barely maintained. A section of the road up
ahead was on their property, and Dustin knew exactly when they crossed the line. The ruts disappeared
and the ride got smoother. "Borrowed a grader a couple years ago and did this section. I offered to do
the rest, but Johnson, the landowner, is a real tight-
ass. He can't stop us from using the road because
we have a right of way, but he refuses to maintain it.
Homophobic asshole."

Dustin couldn't blame Marshall for being upset. "Next time just do it and don't ask. We have right of way. That gives us the right to maintain the access." He settled in for the bumpy ride until Marshall pulled off. "On foot from here?"

"Yeah. It's not too far." Marshall led the way through the undergrowth, and Dustin watched where he stepped. Plenty of nasty things could hide in brush like this, which was part of the reason they wore thick, high boots.

A rustle made them both stop and look around before slowly moving forward. For a second, with the heat and humidity that had moved in, it felt like they were trailblazing through the jungle.

"There it is," Marshall said. The tree had obviously died some time ago and just came down, breaking into pieces when it hit the ground. "The damned thing is probably infested, so we'll cut it up and throw the pieces back in the woods. I don't want to bring it to the woodpile."

Dustin snipped away the wire and pulled it out of the way, rolling up the bad sections for them to cart back to the truck. With that out of the way, they started the saws and went to work. They cut off the dry limbs, and Dustin tossed them well beyond the tree line. They weren't going to last long in this state.

"You were right. This thing is a mess," Dustin said as various creatures scampered from inside the hollow trunk as Marshall cut. He rolled the pieces behind the fence and out of the way, careful not to pick the damned things up. God knows what was inside, and plenty of uglies could hide in there. "What about the rest of it?" A five-foot-tall stump still stood at the tree line.

Marshall turned off the chain saw. "Just leave it. The thing will rot away, and I don't want to disturb whatever might have taken up residence. We need to replace the one post. I suppose we were lucky that way. Will you pull the old one? I'll carry this stuff to the truck and bring out a new one."

"Sure," Dustin said and got to work. The sun was intense, and Dustin unbuttoned his shirt and laid it over one of the standing fence posts, then dug deep into the fertile soil. He pulled out the old post and then dug deeper to prep the hole for the new one. "You know, you could have helped me instead of just standing there."

"I was enjoying the view."

"Is that what we call fence-post-leaning now?" Dustin retorted, still smiling. "Come on. Let's get this in the ground so we can get back and out of this heat."

Marshall set the post, and Dustin tamped the ground around it, using a rod to make sure it was good and compact. Dustin put his shirt back on, and they strung fresh wire across the opening, leaving themselves on the outside of the fence.

Dustin looked over the job, pleased that it was done. "Let's get out of here before every bug in East Texas decides to pay us a visit."

Marshall gathered everything together, and they carried it back to the truck. Once Marshall started the engine, Dustin inhaled the cool air and closed his eyes. There were times when he was so grateful for air-conditioning, and this was one of them. Marshall pressed a cold bottle of water into his hand, and Dustin downed it in a couple of gulps. He sighed and let the cooling air and the hydration do their jobs. "You okay?"

"Just feeling my age a little." Damn, that sucked to admit. "Remember when we used to do shit like that all day and never think about it?" Now the sun sucked so much energy out of him it was frightening.

"We aren't kids anymore," Marshall admitted. "And we can't do some of the things we used to."

"No shit." Dustin got another bottle of water and sipped this one more slowly. "Maybe that's what I'm worried about. I mean, with enough work, you and I can make anything that we set our minds to a success."

Marshall leaned across the seat. "That's what I've been saying."

Dustin slid his eyes open. "But what if we don't have the energy to do that kind of work anymore? We worked out here a couple hours, and I'm wiped. I know some water and a little cooldown will help a lot, but we can't fight Father Time, as much as we might want to."

"I see." Marshall set his jaw and looked forward, putting the truck in gear and beginning the process of turning it around in the tight space.

Dustin groaned. There were times when Marshall could be as stubborn and unreasonable as a teenager. "You don't see shit sometimes," he snapped. "You know that? You see what you want and don't bother to look any further. We can't do the shit we did twenty years ago when we were building this place up from the worn-down ranch it was when we bought it. That's why we have to work smart. If we want to build our place even more, then we gotta do it with something more than just grit that I don't have anymore." Fuck, that was hard to admit.

Marshall threw the truck into Park, and it rocked a little before settling again. "Sometimes you give me a headache. What the hell is it you want?"

"I want to be happy, and I want to make you happy. This rodeo venture is important to you, so I want to make it happen. I'm just saying we can't go through what we did with the ranch in the beginning. You and I can't work ourselves into early graves. That's all." He was getting tired of going over this again and again.

Marshall sighed and sat still. "Thanks," he whispered. "But what's going to make you happy?"

Dustin wished he had an easy answer for him. He tried to think of something that he could say. Marshall made him happy—he always had. But as far as the ranch and everything else, he didn't know what to tell him. Instead, he put his hand on Marshall's thigh and squeezed lightly, and thank God Marshall took the touch as an answer and put the truck back into gear and got them down the washboard portion of the track and out onto the road.

As they approached the turn, Dustin looked over into Richard and Anne's yard. It was empty and still, but just as Marshall slowed at the corner, Richard raced out of the house carrying little Noah.

"Pull in. Now." He didn't even think if he might be intruding. As they turned in the drive, Anne came out of the house holding Oliver's hand. "What's wrong?"

Richard continued getting Noah into the car.

"His temperature spiked really high and…." Anne's lower lip quivered. "We're heading into the hospital in Dallas. Oliver, honey, get in the car."

"He can stay with us," Marshall offered from right behind him. Dustin would have kissed him right there if he wasn't so worried. "That way he isn't going to have to wait at the hospital."

"Is that really okay?" Anne asked. "There's so much waiting, and…." She looked worn out already, and Dustin had a pretty good idea that this was just the beginning for them.

"It's no problem," Dustin said.

Anne thanked him. "I'm not sure how long we'll be…." She reached into her purse and then pressed a set of keys into his hands. "I just don't know, and this way if Oliver needs anything, you can get it."

"Can I get my hat?" Oliver asked, clearly relieved not to be going along.

"Yeah. And you'll need your boots too. You and I have cowboy stuff to do," Marshall said as both parents got in the car.

"We'll call you as soon as we know anything. And thank you. Oliver will be much happier." Anne put her hand outside the lowered window, and Dustin took it for second.

"Don't worry about anything. Oliver is going to be fine. Just see to Noah." He watched as they pulled out, Richard driving as fast as he dared.

Oliver came out of the house with his hat on and carrying his boots, which they put in the truck. Then they helped Oliver get some overnight things.

"Can I play with Pal?" Oliver asked as he raced passed Dustin, who went to lock the house, then returned to the truck. "Is Noah going to be okay?" Oliver was asking Marshall. "What do cowboys do when they're sad?" He got in the back seat, and Marshall made sure he was fastened in the car seat.

"It's okay for a cowboy to be sad, just like anyone else, especially for your brother. Cowboys worry sometimes too because they always care for their family." He smiled, and when Marshall turned around, Dustin kissed him quickly, just because in that moment he had to. Then he got into the truck and closed the door.

Oliver was quiet as they rode the short distance to the ranch. Dustin helped him out of the truck and took his hand. "Come on. Pal is inside, and we have a surprise for you." He unlocked the front door and took Oliver to the mudroom.

"Puppies!" Oliver joyfully clapped his hands. "They peed."

"Yes, they did. Let's take them outside so they can play and I can clean that up." Dustin removed the gate, and the puppies raced to Oliver, bounding around his feet as they yipped for his attention. Dustin took a few minutes to clean up the puppy pads and sanitize the floor where they missed. Then he put down more papers and set the gate in place. "Come on, let's go out in the shade. They need to run around."

Oliver hurried to the door with the puppies right after him, Pal following as well to watch over his pups. Once outside, Oliver ran to the shade of the tree in front, and fortunately the puppies all went along with him. Once Oliver sat down, he giggled as the puppies all squirmed to get to him to play.

"Now that's a sight I never thought I'd see here," Dustin said to himself.

"Why?" Marshall asked as he trudged up carrying Oliver's boots. "They are cute, aren't they?" Dustin nodded. "What's wrong?"

"Nothing," he whispered, his throat aching a little. "It's just… we haven't had kids on the ranch, and it's nice. Little boys and puppies. Do you remember your first dog?" He reached down and gently stroked Pal's head. "I guess I was about Oliver's age when Dad got me my first dog of my own. God, I loved him. There are some things that make a boy grow up a little, and one of them is a dog." He pushed the well of emotion back down as Oliver laughed harder, the puppies starting to settle down, each vying for a place on Oliver's lap.

"Where did they come from? Boy dogs don't have puppies." Oliver's grin was huge.

"Pal found them," Dustin answered. Oliver didn't need to know the cruelty that was behind them finding their place here. The puppies settled down for a few minutes and then started running again. Oliver got up and played with them.

"We should get inside soon. It's danged hot out here."

"I'm hoping the pups will potty," Dustin said. Finally some of them seemed to get the idea. "Oliver, do you want to have ice cream?"

Oliver hurried over, the puppies bounding after him like he had liver snaps in his pocket. Pal followed behind, nudging the straggler forward. Dustin picked up two of the puppies, and Marshall got the others, and they took them inside and put them down in their area. They whined a little, climbing at the gate, with Pal on the other side.

"Sit at the table. Do you like vanilla or chocolate? I also have mint chip and real strawberry." That was Dustin's favorite. "Cowboys like pink." He glared at Marshall, daring him to say otherwise.

"Can I have strawberry, please?" Oliver asked, and Dustin got a bowl and gave him a scoop of ice cream and a spoon.

"Marshall?" Dustin asked, already pulling out the mint. He swore Marshall would eat the stuff by the gallon if he thought he could get away with it. Dustin got his own bowl and sat at the table with the others. "What do you have to do yet?" he asked Marshall.

"I need to get the men to drive one of the herds closer to the pond or they'll overgraze. I'm going to review the way we'll do it with the hands. Do you want to be there?"

"Why don't you go over it with me when you're done? I thought Oliver and I could draw some pictures for Noah." He figured that he'd show Oliver how to draw horses and some of the other animals on the ranch, and then they could make cards and things. "Watch the heat out there."

"I will." Marshall finished his ice cream and took his bowl to the sink.

"Is it cowboy work?" Oliver asked.

Marshall made a face. "It's yucky cowboy paperwork and planning. You stay here with Dustin and do the cowboy drawing and make cards and pictures for Noah. Taking care of family is more important." He patted Dustin on the shoulder as Delta joined them in the kitchen and started cleaning up.

"That's Miss Delta. She's helping us in the house," Dustin told Oliver. "She makes really good cookies and cake." He licked his lips, and Oliver's eyes went wide, like Dustin was so lucky to have someone make cookies and cake for him all the time.

"What do you want for dinner, darlin'?" Delta asked.

"I'm Oliver, and I want chocolate cake." He grinned, and both Dustin and Delta laughed.

"How about cake for dessert? I could make chicken and broccoli? Do you like that?"

Oliver paused. "Little trees?" Delta nodded. "Cheese soup with trees?" he asked.

"I can do that," she agreed. "Is that okay?" she asked Dustin, who nodded. "And you know I make it with a special cowboy ingredient." She leaned close to Oliver. "See, all cowboys love their horses, their mama, and… bacon." She burst into a smile, and Oliver giggled.

"Me too." Oliver grinned.

"Thank you," Dustin added. He was coming to like her more each day. And Delta was one hell of a master of the kitchen, much more than he was. "Go ahead and finish, and then we'll do our cowboy work."

Oliver nodded and went back to his snack. Dustin finished, and Delta snatched up his dish as well as Oliver's. "Are you going to work here?" Delta asked. "I can get a cloth to cover the table." She was already off, and Dustin told Oliver to sit with Pal while he got the things to draw with. He returned with two boxes of supplies he hadn't had out in quite a while. As Dustin got things set up, Oliver sat on the floor, pulled off his shoes, and put on his boots and hat. It seemed if he was going to draw like a cowboy, Oliver was going to look like one too.

"WHAT ARE these?" Oliver asked after he and Dustin had made cards and pictures for Noah. He reached into a box Dustin had placed on the table. "Pretty."

Dustin hadn't meant to leave that box there, but they'd gotten busy and he'd forgotten to move it. "Those are drawings and things I did when I was a teenager."

"Horses," Oliver said. "Big cowboy horses."

"Those are some of the ones I had when I was growing up. I thought that someday I'd be an artist and draw or paint cowboys and stuff." It had been one of those teenage fantasies. He had been able to draw, but he was never good enough to make a living at it.

The front door opened and closed, then Marshall strode in, fanning himself with his hat. "It's a real scorcher." He stopped in the doorway. "Looks like a coloring bomb went off in here."

"We made cards for Noah," Oliver chirped and lifted some of them. Marshall looked them over and gave effusive praise. There was a whole stack of them from Oliver. It was so sweet.

"What's all this?" Marshall asked, peering into the box.

"Uncle Dustin's horsey drawings," Oliver answered, returning to his coloring, head down.

Marshall peered through the box, pulled out a few of the pages, then placed them back inside.

"Do you want me to show you how to draw a horse?" Dustin asked, and then proceeded to give Oliver a basic lesson. The way Oliver concentrated as he followed along was priceless, tongue between his teeth.

"Dinner will be ready in half an hour," Delta told Dustin quietly, so he and Oliver cleaned up all the drawing supplies, and Dustin put his box of old drawings away before he and Oliver took the puppies outside again.

Dustin watched Oliver play with Pal and the pups, laughing and rolling in the grass. His phone vibrated in his pocket, and he pulled it out and answered Richard's call. "How's Noah?"

"He still has a fever that they're trying to bring down, and they're running some tests to try to determine what the trouble is." A worried energy seemed to darken his voice. "How's Oliver?"

"Right now he's in the front yard, playing with the terrier puppies we found a few days ago. I'm not sure who's having more fun, him or the puppies." Oliver giggled as the little ones tried to lick him into submission. "How is Anne holding up?"

"She's with Noah now. I stepped out to get something for her to eat and check in." His voice cracked, and Dustin thought Richard might be breaking down on the other end of the line. "I don't know how much more his little body can take," Richard whispered, most likely around tears and a lump in his throat.

"Oliver can stay here as long as you need. Don't worry. He and Uncle Marshall will do cowboy things." This entire situation tore at his heart, and all he could do was help as much as possible.

"Thank you," Richard said after a few seconds of silence.

"Oliver, do you want to talk to your daddy?" Dustin asked, and Oliver rushed over, the puppies bounding after him.

Dustin let him talk, Oliver's posture going from happy and relaxed to tense in two seconds. Dustin crouched down and petted the puppies and encouraged them to go as much as possible. Oliver brought the phone back, and Dustin spoke to Richard for a few minutes more before ending the call.

"Daddy says Noah is going to be okay and that we can give him his cards soon." All the joy and laughter had left him, though, and even the puppies squirming for his attention didn't seem to help.

"That's right. Your mom and dad took him to the hospital so they can help him get better. Now, let's get the puppies inside, and then we can all have some soup and then chocolate cake." That got a smile.

By the time they got the puppies settled, the table had been set. Dustin and Oliver washed their hands, and they sat down with Marshall joining them.

"Delta?" Dustin indicated the table, and she took a place as well. That was something she didn't seem to understand yet. Meals on the ranch were for everyone... period. Once they were all ready, Oliver put his hands together and said a little prayer for Noah, and then they ate. For a second, the image Dustin had carried for so long in his imagination clicked into place. It was nice—until he remembered, once again, that it wasn't permanent.

Chapter 14

DUSTIN WAS already in bed when Marshall turned out the lights in the office. He had wanted to go over more of the ranch books and finances with him and Anne that evening, but those plans had changed in a huge way. Still, over the past several weeks, Anne had been able to help him get the ranch information into formatted spreadsheets, where it would be easier to load into the program they chose, and Marshall wanted to get that done. So he'd stayed up long after Dustin had gotten Oliver into bed, trying to finish up. But his thoughts got in the way, along with a drawing he'd snatched out of that box of Dustin's. He lifted the drawing off his now largely uncluttered desk. The figures were beautifully drawn, and Marshall could easily pick out himself and Dustin, but what he didn't understand was the third, smaller figure with blond hair who stood in front of a fence, with a house that he didn't recognize behind. A dog played toward the side of the drawing, and horses romped in the background.

"Where did you get that?" Dustin asked from the doorway. Marshall turned to see Dustin in just a pair of sleep shorts—a welcome sight if there ever was one.

"I found it in that box," Marshall answered.

Dustin took it out of his hands. "It's nothing. Just something I drew a long time ago." He seemed embarrassed. "I put this stuff away for a reason, and it isn't important any longer."

"Are you sure?" Marshall knew Dustin well enough to know when his partner was covering something up. Marshall gave Dustin his best "don't bullshit me" look, which usually worked.

"It's just a drawing I made years and years ago. I used to draw things that I saw in my mind or things I'd imagine. I think there's a drawing of a jackalope in that box somewhere." Now Marshall was certain that Dustin was covering something up. "Are you going to come to bed? We have a lot to do tomorrow if we're going to get the cattle moved before they run out of water."

He let Dustin change the subject and lead him toward their bedroom. Marshall paid attention to what Dustin did with the drawing he'd taken because he wanted a closer look at it. Something about that image had gotten to Dustin. Seeing it again had had an effect on him, and Marshall wanted to know more.

Marshall stopped off on the way to clean up and then headed to the bedroom. The drawing wasn't in sight, but he figured it was here somewhere. Still, if Dustin didn't want to talk about it, pushing wasn't going to get him anywhere. Marshall settled under the covers and closed his eyes.

Dustin's phone vibrated on the nightstand, and he snatched it up, the glow of the screen lighting his features. "It's Richard. He and Anne are going to be home in the morning. They have been with Noah for hours and finally got test results." He turned to Marshall. "All his tests came back clear. It isn't the cancer making him sick." Dustin showed him the screen as the bars that someone was typing flashed at the bottom of the screen. *Noah has the flu, but is improving. They want to keep him a little while longer until they are sure he is on the mend.*

Marshall let out a cry and turned to Dustin, pulling him into an intense hug. "Oh my God."

"Yeah." Dustin held him in return. "You just had better not have woken Oliver with your whooping." He buried his head against Marshall, body quivering. "I was so scared." Marshall held him and gently rubbed Dustin's back. "I know we're supposed to be strong. Hell, I rode broncs for years and took more than my fair share of lumps and injuries. I pushed myself until I couldn't take the risks any longer—I know about pain and hurt. But no four-year-old should have to know that."

"I know," Marshall whispered, and he finally understood something about his partner—hell, *husband*. Maybe that was something they needed to rectify. The world had changed, and he and Dustin could get married. It hadn't felt important, but maybe it was what Dustin needed… well, part of it, anyway.

A soft knock came on the door, and Marshall released Dustin and went to open it. "Someone yelled," Oliver said, wiping his eyes, Pal right near his feet. Damn, that was one amazing dog.

"I know, I'm sorry." He knelt down. "Your daddy just messaged us. Noah has a bad case of the flu. His tests for cancer came back good." He flashed a smile. "Your daddy said that he's feeling better and they want to watch over him, but that they will be home soon with Noah." It was like the entire world had shifted in just a few minutes, righting itself in some way that Marshall hadn't even realized was out of balance.

"Really?" Oliver asked, suddenly awake and bouncing from foot to foot.

"Yes. That's what your daddy said." He hugged Oliver and got a huge one in return. "Now go on back to bed, because in the morning we are doing what cowboys do when they are really happy."

Oliver grinned. "Horsey ride?"

Marshall nodded. "Yup. Uncle Dustin and I will take you for a horsey ride. Now go on back to bed and get some sleep so you'll be up and awake for when we go for our ride, and then your mom and dad will bring Noah home. Okay?"

"Okay." Oliver returned to the room he was using, and Pal went with him. Marshall followed and tucked Oliver back in. "Good night."

"Night, Uncle Marshall," Oliver said, already yawning. Marshall guessed he was asleep almost before he reached the bedroom.

"You're amazing with him," Dustin said. "You have so much patience, and you know how to talk to him."

"So do you," Marshall said as he slipped under the covers and turned out the light. He rolled onto his side and slipped close to Dustin. Being with him was so easy, and to think he had let this go because he was having trouble sleeping. Years of separation and just letting things move forward on their own had nearly cost him this permanently. For years his home had become just a house and he had been fighting for something that he'd let drift away—and had been in danger of losing forever.

"Marshall?" Dustin asked in the darkness. "Do you think we're old?"

The question was strange. Yeah, they had gotten a dose of the fact that they weren't as young as they'd once been.

"For what? I think you and I can do anything we want together. Age is a state of mind. Why are you asking?" Marshall didn't move, and Dustin lifted his head.

"I don't know. You and I made some decisions a long time ago, and I've been thinking about them a lot."

"Like the ranch? Is that why you're reticent about expanding?" Marshall asked.

"No. I'm just careful with money and our livelihood." He sighed. "No, I'm talking about other parts of our lives. Do you remember right after we bought this place? You and I sat down, and I remember asking you about horses and if there was a place for a pony. All you did was shiver and look like you were going to either get sick or fall over dead."

"Yeah, because I have no interest in raising ponies. They're mostly for children and…." Marshall stopped. "Is that what this is about? Children?" He wasn't sure how he felt about that. "Do you want to have a baby?" he asked. "I think I'm too old and grumpy for diapers, two-hour feedings all night long, potty training, mixing formula, and God knows what else." He squeezed Dustin closer. "I'd be useless with raising children." Wouldn't he? God, the only role model he had in that regard was pretty bad.

"I'm serious. We talked a little about children, and you had no interest at all," Dustin said.

"I never said that. You were the one who told me that it was something we should talk about, but you didn't seem like it was something you wanted." Shit, that picture. Dustin had said that he used to draw pictures of things he fantasized about, and today Marshall had found a fucking dream-family portrait. "Are children something you want?"

"I think so, yeah. I guess I always did."

"But a baby?" That scared Marshall half to death.

"You're good with kids. Look at Oliver and Noah. They both think you hung the moon and are the epitome of a cowboy. Heck, if you walked through fire, they'd think it was a normal day's work or something. Uncle Marshall can do anything."

"Yeah. But they're not babies." Not that Marshall was totally opposed to the idea. If Dustin wanted a child, he'd figure out how to have one because he wanted to give Dustin anything he wanted.

"I'm not talking about a baby. There are tons of children who need homes. I was thinking that maybe… if we agree, really agree, and that would be after more than one conversation at night, when we're both too tired to move… that maybe you and I could look at giving a home to a little boy or girl who's Oliver's age… or something." The yearning in Dustin's voice was palpable.

"Okay. How about we think about it?" Marshall agreed and tried to push down the feeling in the pit of his stomach that was either acid or enough fear to eat through his stomach lining in a half hour flat.

"MISS DELTA, you make the bestest pancakes," Oliver said, grinning as he shoved in yet another bite. The kid was on this third one, and Delta seemed pleased as punch. Oliver ate the last of his pancake and then bit into some cowboy bacon. Marshall had no idea what made the bacon special, but it seemed to be something between him and Delta, from the way they both grinned at each other.

"Thank you, sweetheart," Delta said and finally sat down. She was starting to make Marshall nervous.

"Can we ride the horse now?" Oliver asked.

Dustin chuckled, and Marshall sipped his coffee. He'd been up for two hours and had gotten some morning chores done. Dustin had helped, so a lot of the day's initial work was complete.

"How about we give all those pancakes a chance to settle?" The last thing he wanted was for that food to make a reappearance. "And you need to get dressed and put on your boots and hat. Then you and Dustin can take the puppies out to play. By then I can have the horses saddled and we can go for a ride."

Oliver was off like a shot.

"That boy has him some real cowboy worship," Delta commented as she sipped some juice. "And that energy…." She shook her head and finished up. "When you boys are done, put the dishes in the sink and scoot. It's cleaning day, and I got a lot of work to get done." The house had never been cleaner, and Delta had found a ring that Marshall had lost years ago.

"Okay. We'll be out of your way in a little while." She turned to the mudroom door, where the puppies sat watching them, doing their best "I'm starved" faces. "I got to clean in there too. I won't have my house smelling like a bathroom." She wrinkled her nose, and Marshall smiled.

"They're getting better." He had already taken them out once when he got up, but the little things still had accidents. They were puppies, after all.

"They are, and the little devils are cute enough." She smiled as Pal loped over for a little attention. Marshall patted his head, and all four puppies whined for their share.

"I'm ready," Oliver announced.

Dustin took his plate to the sink. "Then let's go." He opened the gate, and the puppies scurried out after them.

"Have you thought about kids?" Delta asked. "You're both so good with him."

Marshall shrugged. "If I'm honest, it scares me to death," he admitted. He wondered why he could say this to her and not to Dustin. Marshall knew he needed to try to tell him. "My parents were—"

"Your parents were idiots," Delta interrupted. "Do you think I don't know what they did? This is a small town, and everyone knows everything. You aren't going to turn into your mama and daddy. That isn't going to happen, and if you and Dustin have children, you aren't going to raise them the way you were raised. And if the way you are with Oliver is any indication, you will be a great dad."

He actually smiled. "Do you really think so?" That pleased him. "I like the little guy. He's…."

"What children are. A breath of fresh air and the chance for all of us to right the things our parents didn't do so well." Marshall got the idea that there was a story there.

"Maybe you're right. The ranch feels different with him here," Marshall admitted.

Delta laughed. "That's because it is. It's happier. There's laughter, and everything is new and amazing to Oliver, so you feel it too." She stood and took her mug to the sink. "One thing I know: if you want to feel younger, be around some children. Yeah, they have all that energy and they can wear you out, but they help you see the world as a child again, and that's something we all need." She left the room, probably heading off to do her cleaning.

Marshall finished his coffee, set the mug in the sink, and went outside to find Oliver and Dustin rolling on the ground, the puppies climbing over them.

Marshall left them to their play and got Jackson to saddle his and Dustin's horses. Fortunately he seemed to have gotten over his fascination with Dustin and had settled into his work.

"I hear you're thinking of buying the Winston operation," Jackson said as he worked. "I'd love to be a part of that."

Marshall brushed his horse to get him ready for saddling. "We're talking about it, but that's all right now. But I'll keep that in mind."

Jackson was quiet for a few minutes. "Do you miss it? The rodeo, I mean."

Marshall nodded even though there was a stall wall between them. "I do sometimes. For me it's been a while, but I really did when I had to give it up. But I can tell you that there is life after rodeo and everything else. I don't know what yours will look like—that's up to you."

"Did you know?" Jackson asked.

"Yeah, I did. Because of Dustin. I knew I wanted to make a life with him, and we both wanted a ranch. He and I scrimped and saved everything we earned for those last two years, worked to get sponsorships, doing all that so we would be able to get a place like this when the opportunity came up." Marshall set the brush aside and peered over the stall door. "You don't get anything unless you work for it and figure out how it can happen. Dustin went out on top, and I came close. But it was that hard work, with a plan, followed by twenty years of more work, that allowed us to have all this. None of it was an accident."

Jackson paused in his task and turned toward Marshall. "It was so easy to get used to being the center of attention. But it's hard disappearing back into the nothing that I came from."

"You aren't. You're building a life. If you want applause and to have people clamor for your attention, then go to Hollywood and try to get into the movies. Good luck with that, by the way. If that's what you really want, more power to you. But if it's not, then get on with getting on." Marshall stepped away from the stall wall and finished his brushing. "There's something about this life that's like nothing else."

"I know that," Jackson said.

"I could never have one of those indoor jobs where I worked at a desk all day and stared at a computer. This is what I love, and I get to be out here doing it every day. Yeah, there are times when I really miss the rodeo, but it isn't the crowd—it was the riding and the excitement that I miss… sometimes. And then there's stepping out of the house to the sight of an eight-year-old and my forty-five-year-old partner both rolling on the ground with a litter of puppies. I guess we all have to figure out what's really important." He finished the brushing and saddled the horse. Jackson had finished as well, and they led the horses out into the yard, where two cowboys waited for them.

"Do you want to ride with me or Uncle Marshall?" Dustin asked. Oliver looked at each of them as if trying to decide. Then he stepped right up to Marshall.

"I'll lift him up to you," Jackson offered, and Marshall mounted and made sure he was seated properly before taking Oliver from Jackson and settling him in the saddle in front.

"Where do you want to go?" Marshall asked Dustin.

"How about to the creek?" he offered and then started out. There was a trail that led out that way, so Dustin took it, letting his horse walk.

"See why we need the hat?" Marshall said. "Otherwise a cowboy gets a sunburned face. And the boots we wear are because the grass can cut our legs, and there can be snakes and even scorpions in the grass. But they can't get through the boots. So they make us safer."

"Really?" Oliver asked.

"Yes. Everything we wear has a real purpose. We'd wear chaps if we were going to ride for a long time because they keep our legs from getting rubbed up against the horse. Isn't that cool?" Oliver nodded, his hat bobbing a little. "And rodeo was a way for the cowboy to hone and show off his skills. Bronco busting was part of how horses used to be broken so people could ride them."

"Why would they break the horses? That would hurt," Oliver said. He turned around, his eyes kind of angry.

Marshall chuckled and put an arm around him. "Not break like a glass when it falls to the floor. All horses were wild animals, and some of the ones like what you saw in the rodeo still have that wild in them. Used to be that when a wild horse was tamed, a rider would get on and stay on until the horse wore out, and they would do that again and again until the horse gave up. That was called breaking. Dustin and I don't do that."

"'Cause it's mean?" Oliver insisted.

"It is a little. The last time we worked with a horse, we got him to trust us and then little by little got him used to being ridden. That's how we got so we could ride this horse." He patted the jet-black neck. "He's one of the best horses I've ever had."

Oliver patted him too. "Is that where we're going?" he asked, pointing.

"Yup. And look over there. That's some of our cattle. I bet you can see some of them from your house."

"When are Mommy and Daddy going to be back?" Oliver asked.

Marshall relayed the message to Dustin, who was texting at that moment.

"Your daddy says that they are leaving now. So they'll be here in an hour or so. We'll finish our ride and then make some lunch so they can eat when they get here. What is Noah's favorite food?" Marshall asked.

"Ummm… he likes… grilled cheeses?" Oliver said.

"Then we'll ask Delta to make them for him when he gets here." Marshall passed on the message, and Dustin rode and texted for a few seconds as they continued their slow horsey walk to the stream. Dustin dismounted and helped Oliver down.

"I really like it here. There used to be a swimming hole right up there, but the stream filled it in last winter."

"Can we go in the water?" Oliver asked.

"Take off your boots, and you gotta hold my hand, but we can wade in right here if you want." Marshall helped Oliver with his boots and socks and then stood while he stepped into the edge of the running water. Dustin held the reins of both horses while Oliver splashed and kicked at the water.

"It's cold," he said softly.

"That's because the water starts up in a spring that's in some hills just to the north. So the water comes out cold and then warms up as it goes. Here it's still nice and cool, but farther on it keeps getting warmer." He let Oliver play a little and then helped him out and sat him on a log to let his feet dry before he put his socks and boots on.

"Do cowboys go swimming?" Oliver asked, longingly looking at the water.

"Yes, they definitely do." Marshall shot a wicked glance at Dustin, suddenly remembering a certain cowboy and him skinny-dipping well after dark. They'd jumped the fence to one of the local pools while on the rodeo circuit and quietly swam and made love in the dark water. Marshall pulled his attention back to Oliver when he realized the kid was still looking at him, waiting. "Maybe there's a new swimming hole. We'll have to find it."

"Either that or maybe we could see if Uncle Marshall might consider putting in a swimming pool." Dustin wagged his eyebrows, and damned if Marshall didn't know he was thinking about that same especially good time. He frowned at Dustin because, dammit, he did not need to pop wood in front of the kid when he was wearing these jeans—ones that didn't leave much room for expansion.

"A pool!" Oliver began jumping like a jackrabbit. "Uncle Marshall, you really should build a pool. I can help. I'm really good at digging holes. I have my own shovel and everything." He practically fell into the creek he was so excited. Marshall caught him.

"Whoa, little man. I don't think we'll be putting in a pool anytime soon. But there are plenty of places that we can go swimming. Maybe if we ask nicely, once Noah's feeling better, we can go. Okay?"

Damn, Oliver looked like someone had just taken away his lollipop. He pooched out his lower lip, eyes watery and bigger than the pups'. Dustin turned away, dang him. Marshall could tell he was laughing by his bouncing shoulders.

"Uncle Marshall, *please*?" he asked, just like he would for another cookie. And with those puppy-dog eyes and all that cuteness, danged if Marshall didn't actually wonder where they might put in a swimming pool. He glared at his partner, who tried to seem innocent.

Dustin lost it, laughing out loud. Heck, even the horses seemed to be laughing. Oliver, in contrast, looked completely in earnest.

"How about we see about going to one of the public pools in town? They're really big, and they have water slides." That did the trick, and Oliver was off about water slides and big pools. "Let's finish our ride." Anything to get off the subject of him putting in a swimming pool. He had enough work to do already, and he didn't need to be taking care of a pool.

After checking that Oliver had his socks and boots on, he swung up into the saddle, and Dustin lifted Oliver in front of him. Then Dustin mounted and they started their trip back. "Did you like your ride?"

Oliver settled back against him. "Yes. It was fun. A pool would be fun too, Uncle Marshall." He paused, and Marshall hoped this little discussion subject would end. "Do horses like pools?"

"Not really." He could almost see Oliver trying to reason a pool as a horse wash or something. Not that Marshall could blame him. On sweltering days, a pool would be lovely, except if they had one, no bloody work would ever get done and all he'd want to do was spend his time lounging by the water. Nope, it was way too much temptation. "It's okay, though."

"Yeah," Oliver said. "I like horses."

Marshall tightened his hold on Oliver just a little. "Me too. I used to tell my dad that I wanted to be an old-fashioned cowboy and do everything on horseback. You know, there are some places on the ranch that we can only work on horseback. The four-wheelers can't get there." He loved that about his job. Sometimes there were things that had to be done the old way. "Maybe when you're older, I can teach you how to work with the cattle."

Oliver's hat bobbled, which Marshall took as a yes, and he was beginning to think that he should look into adding a pony to the stable. After all, Oliver and Noah were going to need a way to learn to ride.

IT WAS really hot by the time they reached the yard. Dustin lifted Oliver down. "Take him inside and get him something to drink. I'll get the horses into the barn," Marshall said as he swung down. Jackson hurried out and led Dustin's horse away, with Marshall following.

"Just leave him for now," Jackson said. "I'll get him unsaddled."

"Thanks." Marshall patted his horse's neck, then headed inside where it was cooler. Delta had already poured them all glasses of lemonade and was preparing to send some out to the guys. It seemed Delta was an even bigger caretaker than Dustin.

As they sat there getting something to drink and cooling off, Pal perked up, and the puppies all jumped and yipped. "Looks like your mom and dad are here."

"Good. Lunch will be ready in half an hour," Delta said, heading to the kitchen, while Oliver raced to the front door and pulled it open.

"You gotta come in this way because of the puppies."

Marshall joined the excited youngster, who jumped into his daddy's arms.

"Puppies?" Richard asked. "Have you been having fun with them?"

"Un-huh. Pal found them, and Uncle Marshall and Uncle Dustin are taking good care of them. I got to help, and they pooped in the front yard." He continued talking a mile a minute, then hugged his daddy before continuing right on. "Delta is making grilled cheeses because it's Noah's favorite. I told her." When Richard put him down, Oliver went right to the puppies, let them out, and took them outside.

"I guess he had a good time," Anne said. "I got a kiss, and then he was off with the puppies."

"Can I play too?" Noah asked from his mother's arms.

"You still need to rest," Anne said, and Noah sighed.

"The puppies will be here for a while yet. I promise," Dustin told him. "And once the puppies are played out, you can sit on the sofa and hold one."

"Isn't that nice?" Anne said, looking relieved and tired. Noah rested his head against her shoulder, and Marshall offered her a seat on the sofa.

"Just make yourself comfortable. Delta is making some lunch. We figured you could use a good meal after the last few days."

She sighed. "Thank you." A tear ran down her cheek. "It's been loud and noisy." She paused.

"I understand," Marshall told her. He left the room to give them some quiet time. Delta was setting the table, and Dustin, it seemed, had gone out to check on Oliver and the dogs.

"You didn't have to do all this," Richard said from where he sat at the table, looking worn out.

"Of course they did. Marshall and Dustin were raised properly," Delta piped up as she turned the sandwiches on the griddle. She began pulling things out of the refrigerator, including fruit salad, vegetables, and some her of to-die-for potato salad with lots of bacon. Marshall was beginning to think that bacon was one of Delta's food groups.

Marshall took the chair next to Richard's. "Like Oliver said, we found the pups and are going to care for them for a few more weeks. Dustin is keeping two of them, and we thought the boys would like one of them." He spoke softly. "I haven't mentioned any of this to Oliver, of course, but that's what we thought, if you and Anne agree. The hands are clamoring for the last one, and interested parties can put their name in a hat."

"Really?" Richard said, and for a second he sounded just like Oliver.

"If you agree. Dustin and I know any puppy left with you and the boys will be well loved and cared for." Marshall stood and motioned for Richard to follow. They went out through the temporarily empty mudroom to where Oliver and Dustin played together with bounding, happy dogs.

"How can I say no?" Richard said, and Dustin was just thinking the same thing.

"Can I ask you something? How hard was it having kids? I know you and Anne have been through a lot...."

"And I wouldn't change having the boys for anything. No matter what happens, it's worth it. We're still worried about Noah, but things are looking up.

Still, I'd go through the fire we've navigated ten times over for either of them. Just listen." Oliver's giggles carried on the breeze. "What better sound is there, and what better sight than my son playing like that? I'll talk to Anne, but I can't see her saying no either. These boys need that kind of happiness."

Marshall watched the same scene, but his attention centered on Dustin and the way he interacted with Oliver. The grin on his face, the light in his eyes… and he thought the exact same thing. How could he deny Dustin that kind of happiness?

In a matter of seconds, the path in front of him grew clearer, and Marshall realized what he wanted to do and what would make Dustin happy. The amazing thing? It was what he wanted too.

Chapter 15

DUSTIN WOKE, but the room around him seemed spinny, so he closed his eyes once more. He'd been tired and a little achy for the past three days, since after they brought Noah home, but he'd put it down to working in the heat. After all, with Anne now making some progress on the books and Delta taking care of things inside, his job was outside with the others, and he'd be damned if he was going to let the guys show him up.

"Marshall," Dustin whispered, feeling terrible and just wanting to not feel alone.

"Are you getting up?" Marshall asked, and when Dustin opened his eyes, he saw that Marshall was already dressed. He sat up, and immediately the contents of his stomach made an appearance down the front of him.

"God," Dustin groaned as he pushed back the soiled covers and stumbled to the bathroom, making it in time for round two. "I'm sorry… I…." The problem was that it didn't stop, and he ended up with his head hanging over the bowl as his stomach rebelled again and again and again.

Finally there was nothing left, and Dustin closed his eyes, trying to breathe and hoping to all hell that it didn't start again.

"Delta!" Marshall shouted, and then she was in the doorway. Dustin wanted to die of embarrassment. "Please clean up the bedding and see if the men need breakfast." Marshall was right next to him, getting him to his feet, which didn't seem to want to work. Still, Marshall got him up and pulled off his shirt and tugged off the rest of his clothes. Then he wiped him up and helped him dress in the bedroom before leading him out of the room and down the hall.

"Marshall, I can't." His body felt like it was on fire, and every movement made his guts seem like someone was whipping them in a blender.

"Okay." Marshall lifted him into his arms and carried him through the house and out the door.

"Where are we going?"

"To the fucking hospital," Marshall groaned as they reached the truck. He set Dustin on his feet and pulled open the door. Dustin slowly got inside, and as soon as the door closed, the world seemed to shift into hyperdrive. Never in his life had Dustin been so grateful for Marshall's ability to drive like a bat out of hell, because those wings were flapping at supersonic speed. Marshall even picked up a cop about five miles from the hospital and led the man there as he pulled into the emergency entrance.

Dustin opened the door and somehow managed to climb out and make it into one of the wheelchairs in front. The officer must have taken one look at him and realized what was happening, because Dustin was whisked inside by Marshall with the police officer leading the way and pushing any and all red tape aside.

A nurse asked him what was wrong, and once Dustin told them, they wheeled him into a room and got him in bed. Marshall got his clothes off and Dustin got into one of those gowns. A nurse took all his info, and he explained how he felt. They started an IV a few minutes later, and Dustin closed his eyes because otherwise everything turned spinny again.

Doctors came in and asked more questions that Dustin wasn't really able to answer. Marshall stayed close and tried to help answer the questions when he couldn't. Then, eventually, Dustin was wheeled away for tests and brought back. His insides felt no better, but at least some of the spinning had abated.

"I wish they knew what was wrong with me," Dustin said and took Marshall's hand. "What if I just have the flu or something?"

"You don't," Marshall said. "You never get sick, and even when you do, it passes. You're so weak you couldn't walk. That isn't the flu. Besides, I'm not taking any chances with you." Marshall was right there next to him, and Dustin tried to rest, but his mind ran in circles.

Finally he was wheeled away for another test. He had no idea how long he was gone, but they put him out, and when he woke, a lot of the churning inside was gone.

"Welcome back," the doctor said as he approached in the recovery room. "You had a partial bowel obstruction. We were able to remove it, and I believe your system will return to normal pretty quickly. You were very, very lucky. The obstruction was pretty bad, but it didn't perforate the system."

"I see." He was still so tired and fought to keep his eyes open.

"We'll leave you some care instructions for the next few days, and you may feel tired, but like I said, you were so lucky you got here in time. Now lie still and relax, and someone will take you back to emergency, where we'll have you rest for a few hours before sending you home."

"Is that it?" Dustin asked.

"I think that was enough, don't you?" the doctor asked, and Dustin nodded. "We'll have diet instructions to make sure your system gets working again and to keep any strain off it. But it looks like you're going to be fine." He patted Dustin's shoulder and then left the room, leaving Dustin to drowse until they returned him to the room where Marshall was waiting.

"I'm going to be okay," Dustin said. "It was a bowel obstruction, and they removed it as part of the test, I guess. He said I was very lucky that I got here as fast as I did." He held Marshall's hand. "I promise I'll never complain about your driving again."

Marshall sniffed and kissed the back of his hand. "I'm just glad you're okay."

"Didn't they tell you what was happening?" Dustin asked.

"No. It seems they couldn't because there was no HIPAA thing filled out. So I just had to wait and wonder." He seemed almost as worn out as Dustin felt. "I'm not your husband, so…."

Dustin turned his head on the pillow to face Marshall. "Then do you think that maybe it's time we fixed that?"

Marshall scooted the chair closer. "Darlin', I think it's long past time. I know we didn't think it was really necessary. You and me have shared everything for twenty-five years, and when it got legal, I just didn't think it applied to us. Maybe I'm old-fashioned or just plain stupid, but I never thought of us as the flag-waving, dance-on-floats sort of gay people." He held Dustin's hand tighter and rubbed the back against his cheek.

"I don't see us that way either, though I think the organizers of any float would wet themselves to have you ride on it. Yeah, I guess it didn't occur to me, but that doesn't mean I don't love you enough or anything." Dustin closed his eyes.

"I know you love me enough, and I know you always did. I love you too, sweetheart, so much." Marshall held still, and Dustin opened his eyes because he had to know. Was Marshall crying? At the very least a tear ran down his cheek, and Dustin gently wiped it away. Marshall had been through hell on the circuit, with enough pain to make any man beg to God for mercy. But dammit, Marshall never cried. "I was so fucking scared."

"I know. I was too." He squeezed Marshall's fingers. "So what kind of wedding do you want to have? The kind where we go get the license, have the judge say the words, and just be done with it?"

Marshall coughed. "Hell no. If we're going to do this, then I'm having a full-on horse-riding cowboy wedding. I'm not going to take you to a courthouse to get married like I got you pregnant in high school." Marshall must be feeling better if he could crack a joke.

"Maybe I was the one that got you pregnant," Dustin countered.

Marshall chuckled. "Like either of us has the equipment. Anyway, yes, we'll get the license and plan a proper wedding. I'm not going to marry you on the sly or in secret. You've been the best part of my life for twenty-five years, and I want to celebrate that with all our friends."

Dustin smiled and sighed softly. "Yeah." He liked that idea. He closed his eyes again and tried to rest. He was still very tired, but the blender that had been twisting his insides had been turned off, and now he was tired. The spinning had stopped, and he felt more like himself.

A nurse came in after a while with a number of papers that he had to sign. Then Marshall helped him dress, and after a stop on the way out to get some more papers, they went out to the truck. All he wanted to do at that moment was get out of there and back home.

"UNCLE DUSTIN?" the boys said softly—well, softly for them—as they stood in the bedroom doorway. They both had their hats and polished boots on and looked like little cowboys. Anne had explained that they had insisted when she came over to work through some more of the books with Marshall and that she made sure they were clean to avoid Delta's ire. "Are you better?"

"Yes. I'm better." Though Marshall hadn't let him get out of bed since yesterday except to use the bathroom, which turned out to be a tender but blessed experience. At least things were working and the thought of food didn't send him running to the bathroom.

The boys hurried to stand beside the bed. "We made you these," Oliver said, handing him a stack of pictures and cards.

"These are wonderful," Dustin said, looking at each one. "You made these?" There were even a number of pictures of horses and trees. They were all so colorful, and Dustin made a big deal of each and every one, giving each of the boys a hug. "I think that Delta might have some cookies and ice cream in the kitchen." They smiled and then hurried out of the room.

"Are you really okay?" Anne asked. "I wasn't sure if I should bring the boys over, but they asked me again and again, and they kept drawing more pictures."

Dustin nodded and smiled before pushing back the covers. He was wearing a pair of pajamas that he'd received for Christmas a number of years earlier. Anne snickered, and Dustin rolled his eyes. "I know. It was either these or the ones Marshall got, which had naughty elves on them. I decided the snowmen were fine." He slowly followed her out of the room and to the kitchen.

"You're supposed to be in bed," Marshall said.

Dustin rolled his eyes. "I'm fine, and I'm hungry. The doctor said that I would need to take it easy. I'm not an invalid." He sat across from the boys as Delta dished up ice cream and plates of cookies and set them out for each boy.

"How about some eggs for you?" Delta offered, and Dustin nodded.

"Uncle Dustin, Uncle Marshall says that you and him are going to get married," Oliver said.

Noah grinned. "Are you gonna wear the white dress?" He giggled, joined by Oliver. Clearly they had hatched up their little joke together.

"No one is wearing a dress," Anne said. "Don't be bad or you can't have any more cookies." Man, she had the mom look down pat, and both boys grew silent. "I think it's terrific." She smiled lightly. "Have you picked a date?"

"Next month," Marshall said as he came in. "We're going to have it here. Dustin and I will ride in on horseback, and we'll invite our friends. The ceremony will be outside, followed by a real Texas barbeque." He sat next to Dustin. "Simple, fun, and folks can wear their boots and hats." That sounded good to Dustin—real good.

"How are you settling in with Marshall's quirky book system?" he asked, still holding Marshall's hand.

"It wasn't that bad, and the records were meticulously kept. I found a good program that will handle the books and interface with mobile devices." Marshall rolled his eyes, and Dustin chuckled. He knew how his husband-to-be felt about that sort of stuff. "Think about it. Each head has a numbered tag. All you'll have to do is take a picture of the number and your phone will bring up everything we have, right there. We can use the same system for the rough stock, and if you have information to enter, it can be done on your phone too. No making notes and waiting for later."

Marshall huffed. "Okay. Go ahead and get it set up."

"What about the resources for the possible deal with Winston?" Dustin asked, looking at both of them.

Anne shrugged. "Oh, you have them. Marshall has been setting expansion money aside for years and it's just been sitting there. I want to reconcile all the accounts with the various statements before I give a final recommendation on that front." She leaned forward. "I think the more important suggestion is what kind of business do you want to be in?" She crossed her arms over her chest.

"I don't understand," Marshall said.

"Okay. Right now, you two are in the cattle business. That's what you do, and from what I've seen and in comparing with industry averages, you are at the top of the market and have been for a while. Now, Winston is in the rodeo business." She paused a few seconds. "I'm not someone who is familiar with either one, but they take completely different skills. I mean, Winston raises and breeds animals for their characteristics, right? Just like horse racing out east."

Both he and Marshall nodded. "That isn't something you just walk into. That takes special knowledge, tracking breeding and parentage, sometimes sheer gut instinct… right?"

"How do you know all this?"

Anne grinned. "I had a lot of time to read while Noah was in the hospital, and you asked me to try to help here, so I figured I'd give myself a little education." Damn, she was a smart cookie.

"Mama, can we go play with the puppies?" Noah asked.

Anne nodded, and Marshall guided them outside. "Be careful and watch that they don't run off."

"We will," Oliver called as Pal went along too.

Marshall returned and sat at the table while Delta brought Dustin his eggs and cleared the dishes. Then she went to the front porch, probably to watch the boys while they talked.

"They love it here," Anne said quietly. "I gotta tell you that I was so scared to move out here. We wanted the boys to have some space, but I didn't know what to expect." She smiled. "And what we got was people who treat us better than family and two boys who are as happy as anything." She cleared her throat. "Anyway, back to the business before I forget. There's a lot associated with the rodeo business, including travel and making sure the stock is treated well on the road. All of that."

"What are you saying?" Marshall asked.

"I'm not saying anything other than asking what business you want to be in? You have a niche—a very profitable one—that you could easily expand

and stay within your expert wheelhouse. Do what you do best. You could expand to rough stock and do very well, but I'm willing to bet that mistakes will be made that will cost you money and effort that would never be made if you just expanded what you're doing. I know there's more to this than just dollars and cents, but that's what I have from a business perspective."

Dustin turned to Marshall, almost afraid of what he was going to see. He knew that getting involved with the rodeo was some sort of closely held dream for him, and the thought of taking that away made his belly hurt again. He squeezed Marshall's hand and dared a glance into his eyes. "I'll go with whatever you want to do," Dustin told him.

Marshall didn't say anything and released his hand. Without a word, he got up and left the table and the house, the front door banging closed after him. "I'm sorry. Maybe I should have kept my opinion to myself."

Dustin sighed. "It's not your fault." He knew how hard it was to let go of a dream, and Dustin knew that as soon as Winston spoke with Marshall, he'd had his heart set on getting into rough stock. Dustin could just see that the rodeo cowboy in him wanted to get out and play.

"You two could make a success of it," Anne said.

Dustin nodded, but his heart wasn't in it. "I know. Except the point you made is one that's been in the back of my mind, but I didn't have the words to express it." It was just going to take some time for Marshall to process everything.

"Is Uncle Marshall mad?" Noah asked as he came inside, carrying one of the puppies, his hand under the dog's butt, just like a pro.

"He's a cowboy, and sometimes they have to work things out for themselves," Dustin said, and Noah looked at him like he was speaking a different language. "No. He's a little upset, but he'll be okay."

"Oh." Noah turned around. "I guess no horsey ride." He went back out the door, and Delta snickered as she pulled the door closed.

"Have you thought about a puppy for the boys?" Dustin asked, changing the subject. He was still worried about Marshall, but he knew that Marshall needed to work things through on his own. Sometimes the hardest thing was to just give him some time.

"If you're generous enough to offer one, then…." She took his hand. "You've already done so much for us." She inhaled deeply. "There's just one condition—that you and Marshall tell the boys, but not until next week. Richard or I will get the supplies so that as soon as you tell them, we can bring the little guy home."

"That's a deal," Dustin agreed. "Look, I'm going to go lie back down." He'd eaten his eggs, and now that he had something in his stomach, fatigue had caught up with him. "Let the boys play as long as they want and help yourself to more coffee, or there's lemonade in the refrigerator." He thought of going back to bed, but he got comfortable on the sofa instead.

He sent Marshall a message, but didn't get a response. Not that he was surprised by that. Right now, Marshall was nursing a hurt. It was probably one that he might even have seen coming, but Dustin knew how hard it was to see that a dream you'd held for a long time—even one that you never thought could come true—was in your grasp only to evaporate once again.

Anne moved through the kitchen and then poked her head inside. "Do you mind if I work in the office?"

"Go ahead. I can see the boys, and they're having a good time. Don't you worry."

"Thanks." She disappeared, and Dustin watched through the huge front windows as the boys played and rolled with the dogs. He was glad that Richard and Anne were going to let the boys have one of the pups, and he knew just which one was theirs. He had an extra-large black muzzle and right now was curled up in Noah's lap. He and Marshall would keep one of the boys and the little girl. The last dog one of the men would take. Pal would have other dogs to play with and watch over, and Dustin would eventually need to make an appointment with the vet to have the pups neutered and Sadie spayed.

"Uncle Dustin," Noah called as he came inside, startling Dustin awake. He carried in the puppy and set him on the floor near Dustin. "We thought you might be lonely." The pup roamed a few seconds and then settled down right next to Dustin's feet. "Did Uncle Marshall runned away?"

"No. He just needs to think, and sometimes the best way for a cowboy to do that is out there where he can be out in the sun. It's part of being a cowboy.

Don't worry. Uncle Marshall will definitely be back." Of that he had no doubt.

"Is he sad?" Noah asked. "When I'm sad, I find my mama," he said as though that were the answer for everything. To a four-year-old, Mama could fix anything. For Dustin, it was usually Marshall who tried to fix everything. Dustin really wished he could fix this for Marshall.

"Yes, he is. But he's a cowboy, and sometimes they work things out in their own way." He peered outside to where Oliver was walking toward the door. "Do you want to draw?" Dustin got up and picked up the sleepy puppy, cradling him in his arms as the rest joined them inside. Pal herded the pups back to the mudroom, and Delta did a quick cleanup before settling them down and putting up the gate. Then Dustin got the drawing supplies and set up the boys at the table.

"I'll watch over them," Delta said, and Dustin lay back down on the sofa. Pal lay at his feet, and Dustin closed his eyes while the boys talked between themselves while they worked. Dustin tried not to think of the disappointment in Marshall's eyes, but it was hard for him not to.

"I need the red one," Noah said.

"But I'm using it." Oliver countered.

"Boys," Delta intervened, "cowboys share, and they don't take from their brother. When they do, they don't get cookies." He could almost see her stern glare. He was glad it hadn't been turned on him yet.

"Yes, Miss Delta," Oliver said, and things grew quiet as Dustin's mind began to wander as he drifted off.

"BE QUIET," Anne was saying softly. "Let Uncle Dustin sleep."

"But I wanna say bye and give him pictures," Noah said.

Dustin slid his eyes open and slowly sat up. He almost immediately had a boy on either side of him, each presenting him with more drawings and goodbye hugs.

"Uncle Marshall still runned away," Noah said as though he knew best.

Dustin checked his phone and didn't see any messages. It had been hours. He hoped it was because Marshall had forgotten to charge his phone or something. "He'll be back, and next time we'll go for a ride. Okay?" Dustin offered. Both boys grinned and nodded, and Anne took his hand and said goodbye before they left the house.

"Dustin, your puppies are fixing to pee everywhere," Delta said, and Dustin got up and led the pups outside, where all of them did their business. Dustin praised them before bringing them back inside. He was still so tired, and now he was worried on top of it.

He checked out back, hoping to catch a glimpse of Marshall returning, but he didn't see anything. Disappointed, he sat at the table and cleaned up the drawing stuff from earlier and had a glass of Delta's lemonade.

He wished he had something to make Marshall happy. He'd known Anne was right as soon as she said something, and it was pretty clear that Marshall knew she was correct as well. But that didn't lessen the hurt when it came to something you wanted badly.

The front door opened, and heavy boots hit the floor. "Where have you been?" Dustin asked as Marshall strode in the room. "I tried texting."

Marshall set what was left of his phone on the table. "It fell out of my pocket."

"And a horse stepped on it?" There wasn't much left.

Marshall sat down next to him. "Yeah. After that I rode for a while, and then I came back and got to work. I needed to…."

Dustin took his hand. "I know what you needed. It sucks when there's a dream we've held so close to ourselves that we don't even dare give it voice because we don't think it will ever come true… and then it gets so close, but…."

"I guess so. But Anne is right. If we were going to go into that business, we should have done it twenty years ago."

"Instead, we run the best beef operation in this area of Texas. We have everything to be proud of," Dustin said. "And you know it. There is nothing here that doesn't say that Marshall Brand isn't a rancher's rancher and a cowboy's cowboy." He squeezed Marshall's fingers tighter. "That was good enough for me when I met you, and it's still more than good enough now. As much as I'd like to give you what you wanted and to make you happy… I can't. But if this is truly what you want to do, then I'm with you, and you know that."

Marshall shook his head. "You were right. I actually kept running that through my head, and I figured that you and I could make it work. Then I pictured you and me in fifteen years. I'd have had two ulcers, my back would be killing me, and you'd look like something from *Day of the Living Dead* because we had both been working ourselves to the bone."

Dustin pulled his hand back. "Excuse me. *I'm* the one who would look like the undead? I don't think so. I will never, ever look like Mitch McConnell." He glared at Marshall. "I fully intend to maintain my figure until I pass through the veil to heaven. But I get your point. So we'll tell Winston that we have to decline his offer?"

"I will," Marshall said, taking care of things the way he always had.

Dustin shook his head. "No. We'll do it together. There is no more you or me, just *we*, and it's time we take care of things. I said before that I have your back, and I mean it… in all things." He swallowed hard as Marshall leaned close, Dustin's breathing coming shallow and fast.

"Damn, I really do love you." Marshall slid his hands through Dustin's hair and around the back of his head, then drew him close, taking his lips in a hard kiss that lasted until Delta cleared her throat. Dustin pulled back and then took Marshall's hand and led him out of the room. Maybe what they both needed was a quiet nap, just the two of them.

Chapter 16

THE PAST month had been like nothing Marshall had ever experienced, and for the most part it was amazing. Marshall was still a little sore from having to pass on the deal with the rough stock, but Winston understood and appreciated them giving him an answer so quickly. Still, it had been a dream that he had had to let go of once and for all. But there were other dreams and wishes, and Marshall needed to concentrate on those.

"Tell me why you made me sleep in the other room last night?" Marshall asked as he came out into the hall. They had been sleeping together again for nearly two months, and Marshall had found it hard to fall asleep without Dustin next to him.

"It was the night before our wedding, so it's bad luck for me to see the bride." Dustin was teasing, and Marshall growled at him just for fun. "You look really nice." Dustin brushed some imaginary lint off his shoulder, not that anyone was going to care. He wore a crisp white shirt, a fawn cowboy hat that matched Dustin's, and jeans that had been washed, sized, and brushed to cowboy perfection. He also wore one of his buckles, and noticed that Dustin wore his world championship one, something he had never done before as far as Marshall knew. Their boots were comfortable old friends, cleaned and polished to a proper shine.

"Does Delta have everything ready?" Marshall asked.

Dustin cringed. "Don't let her hear you say that. I told her to hire some help to serve, and she took it to heart. She is running that kitchen and the tent for the dinner and dancing like it's her own little castle, and I swear she will take anyone's head off who tries to storm the battlements. So to answer your question, yes, Delta has everything in hand. Our job is to stay out of her way." He pronounced Marshall completely edible.

Marshall checked his watch. "The ceremony starts in half an hour."

"Yes. Jackson has the horses saddled and ready to go. We'll arrive on horseback. The men will line the route to the altar, and our ring bearers will be waiting for us down front." Patrick had gotten himself ordained two weeks ago, and he was going to perform the ceremony. It was going to be two old cowboys, married by a cowboy, with the next generation of cowboys standing up for them.

"I told you I'd give you a cowboy wedding, and I danged well meant it." Marshall took Dustin's hand. "Come on. We should check things out in the barn and get ourselves ready."

Marshall refused to be nervous as he left the house and walked across the yard. Pal, Sadie, and Russ all hurried over to meet them—their own little pack. Dustin greeted each of them, with the now larger puppies still wriggling for the attention. Then they moved on to where Jackson had their horses ready.

The saddles practically sparkled as the horses stood at the ready. "You did good," Marshall said, patting him on the shoulder. "Thank you. But why are you dressed up like that?"

"He and Willy will lead us over," Dustin answered. "We thought it best, to avoid any surprises." Dustin mounted and checked the time. "Let's get this show on the road."

Willy opened the main door, and then Jackson led Marshall's horse out with Dustin behind him. Once in the open, Willy came up, and he and Jackson led their horses, side by side, around the house and into the back where the guests waited, seated in white chairs under the shade of one of the trees. To the back of the assemblage, Willy and Dustin veered left, and Jackson led Marshall to the right until they were off to the side of the guests. Then each of them dismounted and approached the front of the gathering. Noah stood beside Dustin, his hat off and upside down, the box with the ring inside. Oliver stood the same way, both boys grinning from ear to ear.

"Friends, family, cowboys and cowgirls, we come together today to join Dustin and Marshall in the blessings of marriage." Patrick continued the ceremony that Marshall and Dustin had worked with him to write, though Marshall heard very little. His full attention was on Dustin and those radiantly happy blue eyes, filled with love that Marshall basked in. "Marshall…," Patrick said, and a small chuckle went through the guests. Apparently, he had been lost and missed a cue.

"I do." He held Dustin's hands tighter.

"I do." The boys each handed over the rings and then put on their hats, standing uncharacteristically still for the rest of the ceremony, and they didn't even make *yuck* sounds when Marshall gently cupped Dustin's cheeks in his hands and kissed him.

The guests applauded, and Marshall pulled Dustin to him. "I've loved you for twenty-five years and I'll love you for twenty-five more."

Dustin smiled and rested his forehead against Marshall's. They were married. Marshall had never thought about it before, but he and Dustin were an official family.

"Unca Marshall?" Noah asked from behind him.

He backed away and lifted Noah into his arms, raising the little boy over his head to a chorus of giggles. "Thank you for standing with me. Uncle Dustin and I have a surprise for both of you later." He set Noah down.

"Uncle Marshall, is it time to eat now?" Noah was perpetually hungry. His once bald head now had about a half inch of fuzz, but it was the boy's smile that warmed Marshall's heart.

"It will be soon. I promise. Why don't you find your mom and dad, and they can show you where you're sitting for the dinner." Oliver took Noah's hand, and they hurried out of the area toward the large white tent nearby that was already set up for the meal.

EVERYONE HAD gathered in the tent by the time Marshall and Dustin joined the rest of the guests. Richard and Anne, along with the boys, sat at the main table, as well as Patrick. Delta was busy overseeing everything and looked just as happy as Marshall had ever seen her. Maybe she had missed her calling as an Army sergeant.

Dustin stood, and everyone quieted. "Before we get to the eating, I have a few things I want to say. Marshall and I have been together for twenty-five years." He reached down and tugged Marshall up. "In that time, we've built this ranch and a life together. It hasn't always been easy, but our love for each other got us through the rough patches." He squeezed Marshall's fingers as his emotions threatened to well up. Damn, he hated getting mushy.

"Dustin and I want to thank all of you for coming today." He smiled. "When Dustin and I first got together, something like this"—he motioned around the tent—"wasn't possible, and now I see that anything can happen, even a gay wedding in Texas." Marshall lifted his glass. "I want to make the first toast to Dustin, now my husband, who saw me for who I was even when I didn't know myself. He loved me and stuck by me in spite of my thick head and cowboy stubbornness. Now, that's an accomplishment." He raised his glass, and Dustin chuckled while everyone drank.

"Now that's enough talking. Let's get to the eatin'," Dustin said with a grin, and they sat back down.

Delta hurried over. "You need to go first. No one will eat until after you." She practically pushed them back up, and their table filed over to the buffet. With full plates, they returned to their table. Marshall figured they had about ten or fifteen minutes to eat before they would need to start making the rounds and talking with their guests. But dang, Delta had indeed outdone herself, and the food was amazing.

"UNCLE DUSTIN!" Noah called as he hurried up to where the two of them were two-stepping. Some of the chairs and tables had been moved to the side, and Gunslinger, a western band, had set up shop and was playing some amazing music.

"Yeah, buddy?" Dustin said.

"You said you had something for us."

Marshall grinned. "I did, didn't I?" He caught Jackson's eye, and he nodded and left the tent. "Well, since you and Oliver did such a wonderful job today, Uncle Dustin and I decided that there was something missing on the ranch." He waited a few seconds, the boys' eyes wide with excitement. "See, Uncle Dustin and I figured that since you both want to be cowboys, you'll need to learn to ride a horse." At that moment, Jackson stepped around the house, leading a pony. The boys jumped up and down as Jackson drew closer. "His name is Apple Jack, and he'll be here for the two of you to ride any time. You can only ride when Uncle Dustin or me are around."

The boys were speechless, with Oliver recovering first. "He's for us?"

"To learn how to ride, yes." Marshall lifted Noah. "Come on." When he set Noah on Apple Jack, his grin was huge.

"How about a picture?" Richard suggested.

"Yes. Definitely," Anne agreed. "Oliver, stand in front of the pony. Dustin and Marshall, stand behind." Man, she could take charge fast. "That's perfect." Richard used his phone and snapped images, but it was the one when Marshall leaned closer and Dustin slipped his hand around the back of his neck, drawing him in for a kiss, that they would hang on the wall. The perfect cowboy photograph if Marshall ever saw one.

Epilogue

SUMMER WAS finally starting to wane, and some of the daily heat was letting up, at least to a degree. The highs in the nineties and hundreds had largely turned to eighties, which was perfect weather as far as Dustin was concerned. He paused outside the barn, taking a deep breath as their neighbors' car pulled into the drive. "How did it go?" he asked as soon as the boys bounded out, with Wrangler right behind them. The terrier was growing well and happy to see his siblings.

"Oliver fell off," Noah said. "I wanna mutton bust too."

"When you're better." Noah had been responding well to treatments. His leukemia was in remission, and they all hoped it stayed that way.

"I did better last time," Oliver countered, crossing his arms over his chest. "Mutton busting isn't fair." He kicked the ground.

"You know what cowboys do when they lose?" Dustin asked as he squatted down right in front of him. "They congratulate the winner, and then they go home and practice."

"But we don't got no sheep to bust," Oliver said.

"Then you practice the next time you get the chance." He hugged Oliver. "I know it hurts to lose. Remember, being a good loser and winner is the most important thing." He let him go.

"Can we ride the pony?" Noah asked.

"You remember the rules?" Dustin asked.

They both nodded. "We'll stay in the ring and see if Mr. Jackson can watch us. No fighting, and we have to take turns."

Both Dustin and Marshall had drilled that into them. When Dustin nodded, they both ran off. It seemed the boys had Jackson wrapped around their little fingers the same way they had both Marshall and him.

"You want some coffee?" Dustin asked Richard.

"Thanks," he answered. "How are you able to get them to do exactly what you want with only a word, and at home they'll fight over the stupidest thing?"

Dustin chuckled. "That's the easiest question there is. I have horses, and your boys are going to be cowboys through and through." He held the door as the pack raced up for some attention. Dustin petted all of them, including Wrangler, and then headed inside as the dogs went in search of shade to play in.

"Mr. Richard, I thought that was you," Delta said. "How did mutton busting go?"

"Apparently Oliver fell off right away, and Noah wants to try it… eventually," Richard reported, every inch the proud papa.

"They're out with Jackson to ride Apple Jack." Dustin took off his hat and boots in the mudroom before heading inside. Delta already had mugs on the table. "Have you seen Marshall? His truck isn't out front."

"Not yet. He said he had to take a run into Greenville on some business. But he'll be in soon. I'm just about to take a pan of cinnamon rolls out of the oven. Somehow that man always knows." She clicked her tongue, and sure enough Marshall charged inside and took his place at the table. "See?"

Richard finished his coffee. "I'm going to go out and watch the boys for a while." He thanked Delta for the coffee and left the room.

"Is there something wrong with my cinnamon rolls? No one ever walked away from 'em like that before."

Marshall sipped his coffee. "Richard is on a diet, so I think he's trying to get away from sheer temptation."

"I see," she said, clearly not happy. "Those need to cool a little, and then I can ice them," she told Marshall, who tried to appear innocent but failed. Then she left the room.

"Did you hear the news? The boys just got back from mutton busting. Oliver fell off early. I think they both want to try at the next fair." Dustin grinned as an idea hit him. "That's it. Marshall, we need to add some sheep. Just maybe six or eight. That way the boys can practice." He took Marshall's hand and tried to keep a straight face. "That can be your rough stock."

Marshall growled. "That isn't what I had in mind. Are you crazy? Sheep?"

"Yeah. We can get a little flock. Set up a small contained area. Heck, I bet one of the local sheep farms would work with us if we provided the space for them. Think about it. The boys need a way to practice if they want to have a chance at the fair." Dustin was really getting a kick out of this. "You and the guys could build a gate for them in one of the arenas."

Marshall shook his head. "Let me guess, you got a dose of big eyes and pooched lips, didn't you?" They were both well aware of how those boys had them under their thumbs. "Fine. Randall Meadows has sheep, and I know he provides some to the fair. I'll give him a call."

Dustin leaned over the table. "Thank you." He kissed him and then sat back down. "So what were you doing in Greenville? You've been there three times this week."

"I know." His expression grew very serious and he slid a newspaper across the table.

"This is from almost two weeks ago. You kept it that long?" Dustin asked and scanned the page that Marshall had it open to. "What?" There was a story about the number of children in need of homes.

"I met the director in town visiting family a few months ago, and he asked if I could volunteer. They needed some repairs, and I figured I could help." He reached into his inside pocket and pulled out a picture. Two little boys with huge eyes, big gap-toothed smiles, bright red hair, and freckled cheeks shone back at him. "They're twins, and I met them today for just a few minutes. The boys are six years old. That's Kasey, and the one on the left is Cody. Their mother died two years ago, and they have been in three foster homes since then."

Dustin looked at the picture, his heart skipping a beat as he wondered if he was understanding Marshall correctly. "Marshall, I…." He couldn't stop looking at the picture, those smiles working some magic on his soul. "Can you take me to meet them?" Just like that, a door he thought had been shut opened with a world of possibilities.

"Do you remember a while ago when you asked me if we were too old? At the time I didn't get it, but I do now. And the answer is no, we're not too old for anything we set our minds and hearts to." He slipped an arm around Dustin's waist.

"Marshall, are you sure?" Dustin asked, unashamedly wiping his eyes. "Really?"

"If this is what you want, then it's what I want. Yes. In the past six months, you and I have become uncles to Oliver and Noah, but I think that it's time we thought about becoming parents… together. We have a lot to offer here, and we can sit down and talk about what a future with children of our own could look like." Marshall slid a piece of paper over to him. The drawing that Dustin thought he had hidden in his nightstand. "Is this what you still want?"

Dustin nodded, and Marshall stood, walked around the table, and sat next to him. He put an arm around Dustin's shoulder, and together they started the next chapter of their lives with their ruts gone and the future green, bright, and laid out in front of them.

Keep reading for an excerpt from

Half a Cowboy

by Andrew Grey

Now Available at
www.dreamspinnerpress.com

BEN WAS cold—actually, way past cold. His feet and legs had once been like ice, but now he felt nothing except fear... both ahead and behind him. The fog from his breath hung in the air, and his lungs ached. Ben pulled his coat closed and shoved his gloved hands into his pants pockets, flattening them against his thighs to try to force some warmth into them.

He should have stayed in the car, but no one was going to find him there. He swore under his breath, silently berating himself for going that fast, letting panic override his better judgment. But the car had flipped and ended up far enough from the road that no one would ever see him, especially with the wind that had been blowing earlier wiping away the marks in the snow. The windows had broken in the crash, so the vehicle didn't offer much protection anyway. He needed to find shelter and help.

Fortunately the wind had died, but that also meant that the sky had cleared. That was both a blessing and a curse. The moon shone in the sky, lighting the snow so he could see where he was going even this late at night. But it also meant that the temperature had dropped quickly, and it felt like it was still dropping.

Ben had only one thing on his mind—he had to find shelter. He kept telling himself that over and over with each trudging step through the snowdrifts toward the rise in the distance. He had to make it. That rise might be his only chance to see if there was anything out in this desolate country. He thought he might have seen some buildings this way as he'd driven through.

A shiver began in his back and ran all the way through him, causing his entire body to shake. The Wyoming cold sapped his energy, and Ben knew he was coming to the last of his reserves. His time was running out. He was tempted to just lie down in the snow and give up.

"Shit," he moaned to himself as he took another few steps, the snow not quite as deep as it had been. He made some progress, but the air crackled with the dry cold, and the only sound was the crunch of brittle ice under his shoes.

Step after step, breath after breath, he pushed forward, turning toward a bend in the vegetation… then gasping. A light. There was light.

He hurried forward, fell, then pushed himself back up. Finally he found the road again, which made the going easier. Somehow he must have gotten turned around and gone the wrong way, but there it was. He hurried along much faster now, the pain in his feet returning with the activity. At least that meant they were still working and not about to fall off or something. Ben tried not to think about anything other than the light, which seemed to be mounted on the outside of a low barn or outbuilding.

Shelter—that was all he could think of. He didn't see other buildings, but maybe they were closer to the trees in the distance. He didn't stop to think about it. All his mind screamed at him to do was get out of the cold so he didn't freeze to death.

Ben couldn't believe he had finally broken away from his life of fear. It had taken months to get up the courage, and he had gone in the direction Dallas would least expect: away from the city, away from everyone, out into the wilds of the west and as far from the comforts of civilization as he could get. Of course, it had been his pursuit of those comforts that had gotten him into trouble in the first place. Ben should have known that no one gave something for nothing, and Dallas had offered a life and comforts he had only dreamed about. Definitely more than a kid from Beaumont, Texas, who barely had a high school diploma and who had spent much of his teenage years in foster care, should expect. Unfortunately all the good things Dallas showed him were on the surface, with darkness, fear, and control just underneath. Dallas had been looking for a plaything, a pretty young trophy he could manipulate and show off when it suited him. And Ben had fit the bill perfectly.

He pulled his thoughts away from things he could do nothing about and concentrated on the lights getting closer. And they were, thank God.

The building was indeed a barn, and Ben heard the shuffling of animals inside. He paused at the door before trying to open it, hoping to hell he wouldn't get eaten by a huge dog once he entered.

Then again, anything was better than freezing to death. He pulled, and the door swung toward him, leading to a cavern of darkness. Ben stepped inside and closed the door, standing still as beasts moved in the shadows around him.

Nothing touched him, and he closed his eyes to help force them to adjust. When he opened them again, there was just enough light coming in through the windows to illuminate the outlines of where he was.

It was noticeably warmer inside. He stomped his feet, which ached, but he did it again to rid them of the snow, and brushed his legs off as well. Slowly he walked down the center of the barn, large shapes looming out of the darkness toward him. Horses—they were horses. He sighed a little and inhaled the scent of fresh hay tinged with droppings. Okay, so it wasn't as fresh-smelling as he might have liked. But it was warm—well, warm*er*. He looked around for something, anything, to wrap himself up in.

At the far end, there was a workbench under a window with horsey stuff hung above it and what looked like some folded blankets. They were probably for the animals, but Ben was too cold to care. He lifted two of them and turned to find a place where he could lie down. He was so worn out, his eyes kept drooping and his legs shook. He needed to get warm.

He turned into a dark space with maybe straw on the floor. It seemed dry and clean, so he spread a blanket on the top and lay on it after taking off his boots, pulling the other over him as he shook from head to toe. His feet and hands ached and he was thirsty and still cold, but the blankets helped.

Doing his best to let go of some of his fear, he closed his eyes, willing himself to warm up between the blankets, which smelled like the horses around him. Not that he minded. They didn't seem interested in him, and Ben realized that it was their heat that was keeping the barn warm. At least he was no longer freezing. He figured that as soon as the light came in through the windows, he could venture out into the day and figure out his next steps. He needed to put as much distance behind him as he could as quickly as possible. He had made it this far. If he could get to one of the big California cities, he could blend in, find work, and become a face in the crowd where no one would know he had been a criminal's plaything. No one would be able to find him, and he would be safe. Taking a deep breath, he finally relaxed as the cold that had gripped him so deeply seemed to lose its hold.

SOMETHING DEEP in Ben's dreams shifted. Doors creaked, and he heard footsteps. He tried to figure out where they were coming from, along with the insistent tapping sound that he couldn't place. He burrowed deeper into the blankets, desperate to keep the intense cold he knew was waiting out there for him at bay for a little while longer.

"Would you like to tell me what you're doing here?"

The deep, rough voice cut through Ben's dream and yanked him to full reality. His memory returned in a rush, and he jumped up, nearly tripping over his own aching feet. He had intended to be gone by now, but he must have slept deeper than he intended.

"Answer me."

"I…." He ran his hands through his hair. "I'm sorry. I… the car…. I was freezing…." His knees buckled under him, and he ended up back on the floor of what he now saw was a horse stall.

His head swam, and the world around him seemed to spin as bells rang in his ears. He tried to get up again and this time managed to stand and even take a few steps without falling down, but it took all his willpower to keep on his feet and pull on his boots.

"Those were your footsteps in the snow?" the stranger asked. Ben nodded, slowly turning to face him. "What were you doing to my horses?"

"Nothing." He held on to one of the stall walls. "Just getting out of the cold." Ben tried to remember the last time he had eaten or had anything to drink. "I'll get out of your hair. Sorry for the intrusion." He headed toward the door and pushed it open. It was time to get going anyway.

The light from the sun on the snow was nearly blinding, and the cold took hold of him immediately. He shivered and shook.

"It's okay," the rough voice said from behind him as Ben began to cough. "Marcel, Lucifer, I need your help."

It took all of Ben's will to stay upright as two men, one on either side, took hold of him. He struggled to get away but didn't have the strength. It was happening again. "Please don't hurt me." He fought in mindless panic, but there was nothing he could do but stumble forward in the direction the men were taking him.

"No one is going to hurt you," one of the cowboys said as they helped him into a truck. Ben flopped back on the seat and remained still as the others got in on either side of him. Heat blew out of the vents as they drove a short distance. The men helped him out of the truck and across a small open area into a single-story ranch house. When they walked through the door, Ben wondered if it led to hell. But he was too weak to care. Maybe Dallas had found him after all and this was the end.

Inside was a darker, warmer room, and they helped him lie down with cushions under him and blankets on top, placed there carefully and with soothing words. The man from the barn thanked someone. All Ben knew was that he wasn't standing… and he was so tired. His eyes refused to stay open, but his heart still raced, and he was a jumble of anxiety. Where was he, and what was going to happen to him?

"Drink this, it's warm tea. It will help," the man said, helping him upright.

Ben did as he was told. The liquid felt good and hit his empty belly hard. He held it down and sipped again and again, his thirst taking over.

"Slow down. It's going to be okay." It was the same voice—the man who had snapped at him—but now he seemed gentle and caring.

It had been so long since anyone had cared for Ben. He began to cry, his shoulders shaking as a wave of desperation, loneliness, and helplessness washed over him. "Shit, I'm sorry. I didn't mean to do any of this," he whispered.

"Just drink some more."

Ben did until there was no more, and then he lay back down, real warmth seeping into him. "Thank you," he sighed. He kept his eyes closed because that seemed to make the room stop spinning.

"You're welcome." Footsteps combined with a gentle tapping on the wooden floor retreated and then returned. "Drink some more. I think the cold has dehydrated you, so you need to keep drinking. Then you can rest awhile." He helped Ben with some more of the tea and then laid him back down. Ben pulled the blankets back over himself.

"Thank you," he said again and opened his eyes.

The man leaned over the sofa, adjusting the blankets so they covered Ben's feet, and then turned to him. The biggest, brightest blue eyes Ben had ever seen shone back at him from a face that had seen a lot of life and spent years out in the sun. "You're very welcome. Now rest. I'll make something to eat in a little while." He stood and stepped away, leaning a little on a cane with his left hand. "Just relax. You're safe here." He left the room, and it grew quiet.

The idea that he wasn't going to be hurt, or worse, settled into his mind, and Ben blinked and sighed with relief. Yeah, he knew he couldn't stay here for very long, but some rest would be welcome, and the scent of whatever was cooking in the kitchen had his stomach rumbling. Not that he had the energy to get off this sofa right now. He closed his eyes and figured he would take things one step at a time for now.

After a while—was it an hour, or longer?—the man with the cane returned with a glass of water and helped him drink part of it. Then he set the glass on the table and left the room, only to return with a plate in his free hand. "Go ahead and sit up. Eat a little and you'll start to feel even better." He waited as Ben slowly propped himself against the cushions. Then the man set the plate on his lap and turned to leave once more.

The food was basic: scrambled eggs, a piece of toast cut in half, and a few sausage links. Ben took a bite of egg and then a second. It tasted really good. He drank some more, and then his appetite kicked in and he had to stop himself from shoveling the food into his mouth.

"No one is going to take the plate from you. Just relax and eat slowly. You don't want it to come back up on you." The man sat in a chair at an angle to the sofa with his own plate balanced on his lap. "I'm Ashton, Ashton Covert."

"Ben Mal… voin, Malvoin." He changed his last name to be safe. There was no way he wanted to leave a trail. It was best if Benjamin Malton simply disappeared forever. Besides, these people didn't need to pay for their kindness with the kind of terror Dallas could unleash if he tracked Ben here. "Thank you for all of this." He finished eating and set the plate on the table. Then he drank the rest of his water and lay back down, almost more tired now than he was when they'd brought him in.

"You rest, and we can talk later," Ashton said. "Stay warm. If you want some, there's tea in the kitchen. Water too, of course. Get what you need." He continued eating, and Ben watched him, taking in his weathered features and the way Ashton lifted his gaze sometimes between bites. Ashton's gaze seemed almost hard, like the weight of the world had settled in those eyes. Ben knew exactly how that felt.

By the time Ashton finished eating, Ben was struggling to keep his eyes open. As soon as Ashton left the room, he snuggled under the blankets and fell asleep.

BEN WOKE sometime later. He wasn't sure how long he had been asleep, but the house was silent. No one moved. He slowly pushed back the blankets and sat up, clearing his head. He carefully stood and wandered into the kitchen, where he drank some water and found a plate of cookies on the counter with a note to have some if he liked. *Homemade cookies.* He looked around and marveled at how clean the room was, admiring the pots and pans that hung from the ceiling. That was high-end, expensive cookware for professionals.

The man who lived here was certainly not what Ben expected a rancher to be like. He lifted the plastic wrap and took a cookie, biting into it and moaning softly at the chocolaty, buttery decadence. Ben ate it and took another, then closed the wrap before drinking some more water.

He knew it would probably be best if he left, but he honestly had little idea where he was and no way of going anywhere if he did. His car was useless, probably buried until the spring, not that it was going to do him any good in the shape it was in.

A door opened and nails tapped on the floor. Suddenly Ben was surrounded by a phalanx of dogs jumping and jostling for attention. "If you pet them, they will be your friends for life," Ashton said as he came into the room. "I can put them back out if they bother you."

Ben shook his head and scratched behind ears and down backs, only to get mobbed even more by the motley group of mutts.

"Come on, it's time to eat."

They took off after Ashton and were soon munching away from bowls along the far wall. "Ummm, if someone could give me a ride to a town with a bus station or something, I'll get out of your hair. I need to have someone take care of what's left of my car and...."

"The car was already found and towed. A friend of mine has it, but he says it's probably a lost cause," Ashton said. "As for leaving, I doubt anyone is going to be moving very soon. Another snowstorm is on its way, and all anyone can do is hunker down until it passes. Could be a few days." He pulled out one of the chairs and sat down, motioning for Ben to do the same. "What were you doing out in that kind of weather? Cold nights will kill anything that's out in them. It was near twenty below last night. You were probably less than half an hour from not recovering at all." His gaze bored into Ben, but it didn't come across as bad or challenging, more like intoxicating in its intensity. Ashton was probably in his early thirties, with dark hair and smooth skin over a chiseled jaw, but his deep brown eyes said that he had experienced a lot in those years. Ben shifted a little uncomfortably, wondering if Ashton could look into his soul. What if he didn't like that he saw?

"My car went off the road and...."

Ashton leaned closer, his gaze hard. "Look, you can tell me anything you like to feel safe." Those piercing blue eyes, flecked with touches of green, never wavered. "But you holed up in my barn after an accident you had when you were driving on roads no one would ever have been out on unless they were desperate or in trouble. So which is it? Or is it both?"

His cane dropped to the floor with a bang, pulling his gaze away. Ben took the chance to breathe and come up with a good story.

ANDREW GREY is the author of more than one hundred works of Contemporary Gay Romantic fiction. After twenty-seven years in corporate America, he has now settled down in Central Pennsylvania with his husband of more than twenty-five years, Dominic, and his laptop. An interesting ménage. Andrew grew up in western Michigan with a father who loved to tell stories and a mother who loved to read them. Since then he has lived throughout the country and traveled throughout the world. He is a recipient of the RWA Centennial Award, has a master's degree from the University of Wisconsin–Milwaukee, and now writes full-time. Andrew's hobbies include collecting antiques, gardening, and leaving his dirty dishes anywhere but in the sink (particularly when writing). He considers himself blessed with an accepting family, fantastic friends, and the world's most supportive and loving partner. Andrew currently lives in beautiful, historic Carlisle, Pennsylvania.

Email: andrewgrey@comcast.net
Website: www.andrewgreybooks.com